THE DEEPEST CUT

The Deepest Cut: a MacKinnon Curse novel, Book One
J. A. Templeton
Copyright 2013 © Julia Templeton
ISBN-13 9781480180475

1. Horror-Fiction 2. Ghosts-Fiction 3. Psychic ability-Fiction 4. Self-Mutilation-Fiction 5. Romance-Fiction 6. Supernatural-Fiction

First Edition 2011
Second Edition 2013

Cover Illustration by Kimberly Killion
Cover Photograph by Caroline Zenker
Back Cover by Dar Albert
Print formatting by Tracy Cooper-Posey
Editing by Bulletproofing

THE
DEEPEST
CUT

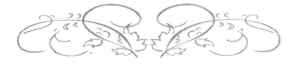

A MacKinnon Curse Novel

Book 1

J.A. Templeton

To Korie Nicole—
Your strength and courage inspires me.
I'm so proud to be your Mom.

Chapter One

My shrink told me moving would be good for me. I couldn't see how leaving behind everything I knew could make my life better. Then again, could things seriously get worse?

"Come on, Riley, it won't be so bad," my dad said, fake smile in place as he slid the key into the lock of the ridiculously huge front door. The old brick inn with ivy clinging to its walls looked like something straight out of a horror movie, and I counted nine chimneys which told me it had been built long before electricity had come into use.

Great. I could hardly wait to see the inside.

With a grunt, my dad pushed the door open and the iron hinges gave a loud creak.

I so didn't want to be here.

The enormous chandelier overhead stirred, sending a creepy tune through the inn I now called home. There was dark wood on every wall, and a chunky staircase took up the better part of the entry. My mom would have loved it here, I thought, my heart squeezing. She had always talked about moving to the country.

Shane, my little brother, pushed past me into the large entryway. He had barely looked at me in weeks. His jaw was clenched tight as he dropped his bag on the wood floor. I could hear the music blaring from his iPod from where I stood five feet away, and as I watched him, he turned it up even louder.

Like blowing out his eardrums would change the fact we'd moved over four thousand miles away from the only home we'd ever known.

I understood why he was pissed off. I mean, *I* was the reason we had moved from an upscale house in Portland's upper west side to this bone-chilling pile of crap in the middle of nowhere Scotland.

Shane removed his headphones and sighed in disgust. "How old is this place?"

"A few centuries," our father replied, searching for a light switch.

"Centuries," I said, an involuntary shudder rushing through my body. Our house in Portland had been built when I was a baby and my mom had renovated five years ago saying everything was out-of-date. This place would need an overhaul.

"Centuries—that's like hundreds of years," Shane said, shutting the door behind him.

Dad flipped the light on and turned to us, grin still in place. "Yeah, it is. Just think of the history here."

More like just think of the ghosts. And a place like this would have plenty of spirits, which is what terrified me—because I can see the dead, and have been able to for a little over a year now—since I was fifteen, when I woke up after a car wreck that had killed my mom. I'd discovered my new "gift" when I was still in the hospital recovering from my injuries. I asked my dad about the old man in a hospital gown who walked up and down the hallway...and straight through walls. I'll never forget the look on his face. The very next day a psychiatrist diagnosed me with a syndrome that had a fancy name, which basically meant he thought I was certifiably crazy. He then wrote out two prescriptions for drugs that made me numb. I couldn't feel anything—except for the pain. Nothing could take away the pain. I missed my mom and I couldn't understand why I could see other spirits, but I couldn't see her.

In fact, I *still* can't understand why my mom hasn't "visited" me.

"I got a great deal on the place," Dad said, breaking into my thoughts.

"I bet you did," Shane said. "They probably saw you coming."

Dad shrugged off the smart-ass comment. "Yeah, it's big, but I wanted a place large enough to store the computer equipment, have an office, and still have room for each of us to do our own thing. Maybe we'll be able to rent out the other rooms to people passing through."

Shane looked at Dad like he'd lost his mind. "You've gotta be shitting me?"

"Watch your mouth, Shane," Dad said, setting his briefcase on a side table that used to be in our dining room back home. Despite the fact I was surrounded by familiar furniture, I felt like I was on another planet.

"You said we were moving near a city," Shane said, tucking his skateboard under his arm. "We're at least an hour away from any city."

Dad's eyes got all squinty—something that happened right before he lost it. "Aberdeen is only forty—or so—minutes away."

"It might as well be five hours for all we'll see of it. We're in the middle of frickin' nowhere." Shane ran a hand through his shaggy blond hair. "What are we supposed to do for fun?"

My fingernails dug into my palms. I hated when they fought, which seemed to be more often of late. The constant bitching was annoying and downright depressing.

"You'll find other kids to hang out with." Dad's voice held a slight edge to it. "I'm sure they've heard of skateboarding over here."

"If I had my way—"

"Shane, this is our home...for now," Dad snapped before releasing a breath. "Let's try to make the most of it."

At least he'd added the "for now" bit. I could barely wrap my brain around the fact this big, drafty inn was going to be home for a while, let alone forever.

Shane walked into the parlor, dropped his skateboard on the couch, and stared out the window. "Mom would never have moved us halfway around the world."

I didn't hear my dad's reply, because suddenly the hair on my arms stood on end. I straightened. I knew the old inn would be full of ghosts.

Maybe this time it would be my mom.

With my heart racing nearly out of my chest, I turned my head and could see the spirit standing just off the entry—a tall figure lingering in the shadows. Disappointment washed over me. It was a man, not a woman.

Not my mom.

I knew better than to make eye contact. Once I did, the spirit never left me alone.

"Why couldn't you have waited to take this new job until we graduated?" Shane asked. "I wish I were eighteen. I'd be so out of here."

A nerve in Dad's jaw jumped. "But you're fifteen, Shane, not eighteen. You'll just have to tough it out with me for three more years."

Shane glanced over at me, anger brimming in his blue eyes. There had been a time we'd been close, but after Mom died everything had changed, and now I felt the distance more than ever.

I cleared my throat. "Dad, where's my room?"

"Up the stairs, take a right, first door on the left. Shane, your room is at the top of the stairs, take a left, and it's the first right."

Anxious to be alone, I headed up the creaky stairs to hide away in my room, praying the ghost didn't follow.

"Nice, Shane. You know what your sister's been through."

"I lost my mom, too," Shane said defensively. "Just because I wasn't in the car with her when she died…"

I blocked out their voices and resisted the urge to take the steps two at a time.

Shane followed behind me, the ghost fast on his heels.

Forcing myself to remain calm, I took a right at the top of the steps, then pushed open the first door on the left.

I wrinkled my nose. The room, filled with my familiar furniture, was huge and smelled musty. There was a large window covered by hideous gold velvet drapes that might just be as ancient as the inn itself. I noticed two doors, one leading to a closet, and the other to my very own attached bathroom. Pleasantly surprised, I opened the door. There was a pedestal sink with a mirrored medicine cabinet above it, and a tub/shower with a basic white shower curtain hanging from silver loops.

Though the bathroom wasn't huge by any means, it was mine, and I was glad I wouldn't have to venture into the hallway at night to use the bathroom.

I crossed the room and looked out the only window to find I had a perfect view of a reddish stone castle sitting on a grassy knoll surrounded by tall trees. It wasn't a Cinderella castle by any means, but there were elements of the whimsical about it with its turrets and spires, and yet something oddly menacing too. Dark and depressing—kind of like my life.

I caught my reflection in the glass and was shocked at the circles beneath my green eyes. My cheeks even looked hollowed out from all the weight I had lost this past year. I looked fragile, and even more, I felt fragile.

Loud music boomed from next door, startling me. Dad yelled at Shane to turn it down, and of course, he only turned the music up louder.

I leaned against the windowsill, my forehead resting against the cool glass. My gaze shifted to the castle again. There was something about that castle that both repelled and intrigued me—almost like it called out to me.

The air around me suddenly turned cold, and I felt someone standing behind me. It's a sensation I'll never get used to, and I feared turning around, afraid of what—or rather *who*—I would find. I felt an odd burning in my chest, and I could barely breathe, like something was stuck in my throat. From the time I saw that first ghost, I learned that I could physically feel what they had at the time of their death. The sensation usually lasted only seconds, but that was long enough for me to get the general idea of how they passed. I couldn't tell if this guy had been strangled or what...but the pain grew more intense and a wave of nausea hit me.

Swallowing past the lump in my throat, I said my brother's name out loud, knowing full well he wouldn't hear me over the pounding bass that even now vibrated the floor beneath my feet.

An icy hand touched my shoulder. I closed my eyes, willing the spirit to go away.

It didn't.

I turned my head to the left just the slightest bit, and saw a guy standing directly behind me. He appeared to be a little older than me, with shiny dark hair that brushed his broad shoulders. Though I wanted to look him straight in the eye, I didn't. I couldn't let on that I could see him. "Shane," I yelled, louder this time.

I had only befriended one other ghost in the hope she'd help bring my mom around. It had been the biggest mistake of my life. The old woman had hounded me nearly every waking hour until finally I ignored her, pretending to no longer hear or see her. It worked, even if it took weeks for her to realize as much. She never bothered me again.

My bedroom door whipped open abruptly and the spirit disappeared just as quickly as it had appeared. "What's wrong?" my dad asked, concern in his eyes. I knew that look. That *oh my God, my daughter's losing her mind* expression. The same expression he'd had when I told him I could see ghosts. I couldn't tell him the truth, especially since I'd lied and told him months ago that I didn't see spirits anymore.

I brushed a trembling hand through my hair. "Nothing."

"You're so pale." He walked over to me and pressed his palm against my forehead. It felt strange to have him touch me. I had pulled away from him so much, both mentally and physically these past months, and yet a huge part of me wanted to bury my face in his chest and tell him how much I needed him. How sorry I was that I had changed all of our lives. How much I wanted to go home.

"It doesn't feel like you have a fever," he said, his hand dropping back to his side.

"I just have a headache."

"You need an aspirin?"

I shook my head. "No, I just need a nap."

"I'll tell Shane to turn that racket down."

"No, don't. He's already mad at me...and I don't blame him."

His brows furrowed. "What do you mean?"

"Dad, I know I'm the reason we moved to Scotland. All the trouble I've—"

"Riley," he said, lifting my chin with gentle fingers. His eyes were sad, and I knew he missed the relationship we had once shared. "I accepted this job because it was an opportunity of a lifetime, and I felt this move would be good for all of us, your brother included. He wasn't exactly hanging out with a good group of kids back home."

When I didn't respond, he sighed heavily. "I just want us all to be happy, hon. I think we can be...if given the chance."

I didn't have the heart to tell him that being happy would require bringing Mom back.

"So, what do you think of your room?" He had a hopeful expression on his face. I'd noticed on the trip here that, like me, he had lost weight, his pants now hanging off his thin frame. Even his face looked haggard, and his once sandy-blond hair had turned gray at the temples. Sometimes it was hard to remember that he was grieving just as much as I was.

"I like it, especially the bathroom."

He grinned. "Nice, huh? Every bedroom has one. I suppose that's one of the perks of buying an inn." As an awkward silence followed, he checked his watch. "Well, I've got to get going. I called Miss Akin and she said she'd be here in about ten minutes."

Miss Akin was the babysitter/housekeeper/cook Dad had hired to keep an eye on Shane and me while he was working fifteen-hour days. "Dad, we're old enough to take care of ourselves."

His brows rose nearly to his hairline. "I'll be working long hours and I don't want the two of you to be alone. Plus, it's Miss Akin's job to take care of the place. I want you focusing on being a kid."

I had high hopes that Miss Akin, hence the *Miss*, would be a young, hip twenty-something, punk rock Scottish chick who would breathe new life into this place, but with my luck, she'd be an old spinster who would make my life even more unbearable.

As he headed for the door, I asked, "When will you be home?"

He checked his watch again. "Not too late."

Not too late meant we'd most likely see him tomorrow.

Chapter Two

iss Akin was about seventy years old with gray hair held back in a tight bun, wide hazel eyes, and a high-pitched laugh that reminded me of a witch's cackle. Nearly as round as she was tall, she wore a white apron over a floral dress, nylons, and loafers. There was a grandma-like quality about her I liked, and at the moment she lingered in my bedroom doorway.

"Is there anything I can get you, dear?" she asked, her "you" sounding more like "ye"—which seemed to be the norm in Scotland.

"No, I'm fine. In fact, I think I'll take a walk and get some fresh air."

Her lips curved into a wide smile. "Don't wander off too far."

"Miss Akin, I'm sixteen, not twelve."

Her eyes twinkled. "Ah, sixteen. Such a brilliant age, full of wonder...and boys."

I rolled my eyes and she giggled like a girl.

"Oh, and Riley dear—dinner will be at half past five, so kee
in mind while you are out explorin'."

She shut the door, and I took a few minutes to pull my blonde
hair up into a sloppy ponytail, and change from sweats to jeans and a
hoodie. The ghost hadn't returned since my father's abrupt entrance
and I was relieved. I hoped he got the idea I couldn't see him, and
therefore, he was wasting his time haunting my new home.

Needing to clear my mind, I checked to make sure I had everything I needed and headed out the door.

Once outside, I started across the field dotted with heather, and
headed straight for the castle.

I felt like I was living somebody else's life. Everything was so un-
familiar, so opposite of Portland, where I'd been born and raised. I
was unused to so much quiet. It was almost unsettling not to hear
kids playing, horns honking, or just the sounds of the city. I wondered how long it would take before I went crazy.

I passed by an old cemetery surrounded by a rock wall. A flock of
birds flew from a tree, nearly startling me out of my skin. They
soared above the cemetery and landed on top of an old mausoleum.
Hundreds of tombstones of various shapes and sizes littered the
graveyard, the majority being crosses and giant slabs, some of which
were leaning over and crumbling. The place was old, and I wondered
just how far back the dates on the tombstones would go. Not that I
planned on investigating. I hated cemeteries. My mother had been
cremated and her ashes were in a mahogany box that my dad kept in
his bedroom. I know it sounds weird but I found it strangely comforting to know she wasn't in the ground.

A car blew past me, missing me by inches, and pulling me abruptly back to the present.

The castle's driveway was blocked by a large chain. Obviously the owners were only concerned about cars driving in, and not foot traffic. I inched under it easily enough.

I walked through the tall trees and looked up at the castle where the blue and white Scottish flag waved from the ramparts. The castle was more intimidating up close than from a distance, and I felt a strange compulsion to run, mixed with an almost need to explore it, but I stayed rooted to the spot. There were no cars around, and I wondered if it was a private residence or one of those castles owned by a trust. Though a part of me wanted to check it out, I didn't dare. Honestly, I didn't have the guts. Plus, I didn't come here for a tour.

I pulled the small matchbox out of my pocket. My hand shook as I slid the box open and unwrapped the gleaming new blade within. Sitting on a soft patch of grass beneath a giant oak tree, I looked around to make sure I was alone.

Seeing no one, I rolled up the leg of my jeans and slid my sock down. I took a deep, steadying breath, released it, and before I could talk myself out of it, I ran the blade slowly against my skin. I winced at the pain, and watched as blood beaded against the blade. I cut further, deeper, and the release came, taking with it the anxiety and frustration that had been building within me for weeks.

Blood streamed down my ankle, soaking into my white sock. I set the blade aside and mopped at the crimson stream with a tissue. Damn, I had cut deeper than intended. Reaching into the matchbox, I pulled out a Band-Aid.

I closed my eyes and pushed away the guilt and disgust that always came with cutting. I had "officially" quit self-mutilating two months ago, but the move had pushed me over the edge, I reasoned.

"Bloody hell, what are you doing, lass?"

I gasped, horrified to hear I was no longer alone. How could I possibly explain what I'd been up to?

Slowly I turned to find a guy watching me with disbelief in his piercing blue eyes. That disbelief quickly turned to bewilderment as our gazes locked and held.

Oh my God. It was the ghost from the inn...and he had followed me here.

Chapter Three

You *can* see me," the ghost said in a thick Scottish accent. It wasn't a question.

I looked away, but it was too late. He knew I had seen—and heard him. He was pumped. I could see the excitement in his eyes.

I was so screwed. What had I done? Why had I reacted? This was so not the way I wanted to start off in a new town. Now every spirit in Braemar would be on my doorstep wanting to talk to me.

Pissed at myself, I took the Band-Aid out of the wrapper and placed it over the cut, my mind racing. With a trembling hand, I put the blade back into the bloodied tissue and into the matchbox, and shoved it in my pocket.

Pulling up my sock, I felt the blood flow over and around the bandage, seeping into my sock and into my shoe. Only one person had ever asked me about cutting, and that had been Becca, my best friend since third grade. During P.E. one day last year, Becca had seen the scab on my leg and asked what had happened. I saw the concern in her eyes, and when I told her I'd fallen and scraped myself, I could tell she didn't buy it.

"What's your name?" he asked, looking like he wanted to hug me.

I stood so fast, I got a head rush and had to grab on to the tree for support.

"Are you well?" he asked, sounding concerned.

The lightheadedness passed and I pushed away from the tree, wanting to get as far away as fast as I could. Why had I cut out in the open? What an idiot. I should have waited until tonight, after everyone was asleep. I was sure there was a lock on my bathroom door.

Then again, it's not like a lock would keep a ghost out.

"Say something." The ghost followed beside me. "I know you see me. You looked right at me for feck's sake. Speak to me, lass. Say something." He was starting to sound desperate.

As desperate as I was to get away from him.

I pulled the hoodie up over my head, hoping he would just go away.

He didn't.

I rushed from the trees, onto the main road, and nearly into the path of an oncoming car that had to swerve to avoid hitting me.

Jesus, what was wrong with drivers here?

"Watch where you are going, lass. You could get yourself killed."

If only he knew how little I cared about living.

"What is your name?"

He was seriously getting on my nerves.

The ghost stayed with me, and even moved ahead, and then he came to an abrupt stop in the middle of the road.

I walked straight through him and smiled inwardly as he cussed under his breath. He was determined—I'd give him that. He was back beside me in seconds, staring at me.

My footsteps faltered as I came closer to the inn. As much as I'd like to escape to my room and crash out, I couldn't face the inquisitive Miss Akin, or my moody brother for that matter. Plus, I had a feeling Mister Annoying here wasn't about to leave me alone. I left the main road and veered off, onto the grass and toward the river, hoping the ghost would get the hint I didn't want his company.

"I have no intention of leaving, if that is what you are hoping I will do," he whispered in my ear. "I shall stay with you every second until you acknowledge me."

He was so close I felt his icy breath on my neck.

A small car packed with teenagers drove by and I quickly averted my gaze. The car slowed and I kept walking, away from the road, and over a small, grassy knoll. As promised, the ghost stayed with me.

I found a place on the river's edge. I glanced over my shoulder to see the inn, which gave me some comfort. Not that I felt in danger from the ghost at my side.

He started whistling, and I knew he did it to get under my skin.

Sitting on a flat stone, I leaned over and picked up a few small rocks. I threw them into the river, one by one, and as promised, the ghost didn't budge. In fact, he stared at me. Honestly, I wanted to stare back. In that fleeting moment at the castle when I looked at him, I couldn't believe how hot he was with his long dark hair and brilliant blue eyes.

I'd also noticed his bizarre clothing—snug, thigh-hugging black pants, and a pirate-looking shirt that opened in a V at the neck and showed part of his wide chest. Knee-high boots finished off the outfit. Given the clothing, I wondered how long he'd been wandering the earth as a spirit.

"Talk to me, lass. I swear to you that I will not harm you."

I liked his deep voice and sexy accent...even if he did speak like he was a Renaissance Faire regular.

"And if you do not speak to me, I will not leave your side...ever. I can chatter all hours of the day and night, if you like."

My better judgment told me to keep my mouth closed, and yet a part of me was curious. I'd never met a ghost close to my age before. I ran a hand down my face in indecision.

"Or, I can continue to whistle, or perhaps you prefer singing..."

Before I could talk myself out of it, I turned and looked directly at him.

My heart skipped a beat.

He was movie-star gorgeous, his eyes even more amazing than I remembered from that first glimpse. The brilliant blue orbs were framed by long, thick lashes any girl would kill to have, and he had high cheekbones and nice, full lips. Tall and broad shouldered, he made me feel all fluttery inside.

As I continued to stare at him, his blue eyes mirrored the same shock as when I'd first looked at him.

"My name's Riley Williams, and yes—I see you."

"Riley Williams," he whispered, his lips curving into a grin that made my thighs tighten. "Do you know I have not conversed with anyone for over two hundred years?"

I couldn't even imagine going a day without talking to someone, but two hundred years? "That's a long time," I said, and he laughed under his breath.

"Yes, it is. By the way, my name is Ian MacKinnon."

"It's nice to meet you, Ian."

"And it's a pleasure to meet you, lass." He tilted his head slightly as he watched me, and I shifted under that intense stare, wondering exactly what he was thinking...especially since he knew my secret. "What is your age, Riley?"

"Sixteen. How old are you?"

"Nineteen."

"So how did you die?" I blurted, before he could start drilling me about why I'd been cutting myself.

"I was poisoned."

Talk about a miserable way to go. Suddenly, I remembered the way my throat and chest had burned earlier when he'd come into my room. The pain had been intense. "So...why would someone poison you...or was it an accident?"

"My death was no accident. A servant who worked for my family is the one responsible."

I'd heard of ghosts who had been murdered, hanging around because their souls were restless, and I wondered if that was the case with Ian. "So is that why you stay here?"

"No, I stay here because I am cursed to roam these lands for all eternity," he said matter-of-factly.

"Cursed?" I laughed, wondering if he was trying to feed me a load of bullshit, but could tell by the look on his face that he was serious. I had no idea that curses were real. Then again, not so long ago I hadn't believed ghosts were real either.

His gaze lingered on my face, making me uncomfortable. I hadn't even bothered with makeup. "When exactly did you die?"

"Seventeen hundred and eighty-six."

Well, that would explain the clothes. "Wow, you're really old... although I think my house might just be older than you."

His top teeth dragged along his bottom lip, and my stomach did a little flip. Even his teeth were perfect, white and straight, which was surprising given he came from a time before braces and white strips. "When we had hunting parties, many of our guests would stay at the inn if there was not room for them at the castle."

"The castle?" My heart missed a beat. "*You* lived in the castle?"

He nodded, pride shining in his eyes. "Yes, I did with my father, my mum, my brother, and two sisters."

"Are they cursed as well?"

"No, I am alone."

How depressing. I couldn't imagine being alone for so many years, wandering day after day with no one to talk to. "And no one could see you?"

"There have been times when the living could see me, but they usually are so scared, they scream or yell. You are the first person who has actually acknowledged me."

He was becoming more translucent, something I had noticed with the old lady ghost when she came around. At first she would look as human as me, but the longer she stayed, the more her energy began to fade, and so did her form, until she disappeared altogether. Strangely enough, I didn't want him to go. It was nice to have someone my age to talk to.

His gaze shifted down to my ankle. "You do not have to answer me if you don't wish to, but I am curious...why did you hurt yourself?"

The question surprised me, and as uncomfortable as it made me feel, I answered him. "I was in the car with my mom when she died."

He sat up and rested his forearms on his knees.

"My life hasn't been the same since, and to deal with the pain, I cut myself."

He frowned, and I could tell he had questions, but he remained quiet...for all of two seconds. "Explain what you mean?"

I didn't see condemnation in his eyes—just a need to understand.

"When I cut it's like a release, a way to get my frustration out."

"Why would hurting yourself help ease the pain you feel inside?"

For some reason his desire to understand made me like him even more, but giving an explanation of why I cut was tough. I didn't even really understand why I did it. I took a deep breath. "Well... when I cut the skin, and feel the pain...and see the blood—it's like I'm letting out this loud scream."

I felt Ian's cool fingertips on my hand, the slightest touch, but oddly, it felt wonderful and comforting in a way that surprised me. It had been a long time since I'd had a friend to talk to. Our gazes caught and held, and I saw no judgment in those blue eyes, or even sympathy...just understanding. Honestly, I never thought I'd find solace in a ghost's touch, and my throat grew tight as he continued to watch me.

"Have you always been able to see spirits?"

I shook my head. "No. A year ago—when I woke from the wreck, that's when I saw my first ghost. Oh, and by the way, I saw you earlier at the inn," I admitted, wanting to return to a less depressing topic.

He grinned, exposing deep dimples I hadn't noticed before. How sad he had died so young. What a waste. "You did not let on that you could see me."

I wiggled my brows. "That was my intention. Then again, I didn't expect you to follow me to the castle either."

His lips quirked slightly. "I was curious about you and your family. The inn has been empty for years now."

"I can see why," I said before I could stop myself.

He laughed—a deep, rumbling sound that sent a spike of pleasure through me. "Despite your lack of enthusiasm, I am glad you are here, Riley."

And oddly, in that moment, I was glad I had come to Braemar

too.

"Riley!"

I looked over my shoulder and saw my brother standing nearby, watching me like I'd grown another head. I knew he had heard me talking to Ian, or rather, to myself. Knowing how bad it looked, I felt my face turn hot, and I came slowly to my feet, brushing at my butt, trying to think of what to say to explain myself.

"I shall see you soon, Riley," Ian said, fading faster by the second.

Shane's gaze scanned the vicinity. "Miss Akin sent me to find you. She has dinner ready."

"Dinner?" I said absently.

"You've been gone for almost two hours."

Two hours? It hadn't felt like two hours. The time had flown by.

"All right, I'm coming." I refrained from looking over my shoulder one more time to see if Ian was still there.

Chapter Four

I awoke at eight thirty to the sound of Miss Akin humming.

"It's about time you are up, love. You need to get ready to register for school."

I sat up in bed. School? "But school doesn't start for weeks." The very thought of starting a new school made me sick to my stomach, especially since my grades had taken a serious dive in the past year.

"Yes, but you register for your classes today."

Could my life suck more? I wasn't ready to face my peers, who undoubtedly would completely pick me apart.

"Is my dad here?" I asked, even though I already knew the answer. Work was his life. Always had been, always would be. Moving to Scotland wouldn't change that.

"No, he left about seven. Said he'd see you tonight." She set a pile of folded laundry on my dresser and clapped her hands together. "You had best get moving. I know how young women are when it comes to primping."

She so didn't know me. I wasn't the primping type. I needed thirty minutes to get ready, from the time I entered the shower, to the time I walked out the door. I was hungry though, and my stomach chose that moment to growl.

Miss Akin smiled. "I tell you what—you get in the shower and I'll set to work on making you breakfast. How does eggs and haggis sound?"

"Haggis?" I'd heard horror stories about the Scottish version of sausage, made of sheep heart and other parts. "No thanks, but I wouldn't mind some eggs and toast."

Miss Akin looked a little disappointed I wasn't taking her up on the haggis, but I couldn't eat anything that got my sensitive gag reflex going. "Is Shane up?"

"Yes, and already gone."

Now that surprised me. Shane usually slept until noon.

"He said something about seeing you over at the school." She picked up my dirty socks and frowned. "Did you cut yourself, love?"

My stomach clenched. Normally when cutting I was careful, hiding the blood by either tossing out or washing the soiled clothes myself, but in my excitement after meeting Ian, it had completely slipped my mind. "No. Why?"

"There's dried blood on your sock."

"I must have cut myself shaving."

"My goodness, it must have been quite a gouge to leave such a stain. Be careful next time, my dear."

"I will," I said, scrambling off the bed. I pulled on some sweatpants and opened up the curtains, looking out at the castle. I was even more curious about the castle now that I knew Ian had lived there. I admit I wanted to know more about him, and already couldn't wait to see him again. "Miss Akin, is the castle open to the public?"

"Usually sections of the castle are open for visitors this time of year, but the family who owns it is on holiday, and while they're away they've decided to tackle some much-needed renovations. Only the construction crew is allowed in for now."

Disappointed, I asked, "When does the family return?"

"The end of the month, I believe. Just in time for school."

I had no intention of waiting weeks to see the castle.

"You get in that shower and I'll get to making your breakfast," she said, nudging me toward the bathroom.

Within thirty minutes I had showered and dried my hair. I had no idea what was in fashion in Braemar, Scotland, so I thought I'd play it safe with name-brand jeans, a baby-blue T-shirt, and tennis shoes. My hair wouldn't cooperate, so I pulled it up into a high ponytail, and grabbed a lightweight jacket out of my closet.

I found Miss Akin in the kitchen, humming to herself. I wolfed down a piece of toast, wanting to get to the school early, and hopefully, find Shane.

I left the house and crossed the road, passing by a restaurant that was packed and a store where a few old men sat out on a bench, talking and smoking. On every street corner, flower baskets full of colorful blooms hung from old-fashioned lampposts. I hated to admit it, but the little town had a charm most cities lacked. I was used to strip malls and subdivisions, not quaint houses on huge lots, and miles upon miles of open green space.

I walked over the ancient stone bridge, my fingers brushing the polished iron railing as I looked down at the river, remembering the expression on Ian's face yesterday when I'd turned to him and told him I could see him. There was a part of me that questioned befriending a ghost. Let's face it, the possibilities of someone aside from my brother, Dad, and Miss Akin seeing me talking to myself were pretty high. If I wasn't careful, I could end up in a mental hospital or, at the very least, forced to take those horrible meds again.

I heard a familiar voice and saw Shane step out of a store, followed by two other boys, both of whom carried skateboards. When Shane looked my way, he actually waved and walked toward me. "Riley, this is Richie and Milo. Guys, this is my sister, Riley."

"Hey, Riley," the boys said in unison, checking me out hard, especially Milo whose eyes were practically glued to my boobs.

"Hey," I said with a smile.

Richie had red hair he wore back in a low ponytail, a navy and gray V-neck sweater, and jeans that had seen better days. Milo had a lip ring, and what I assumed to be dyed black spiky hair, since his eyes were hazel and his skin really pale. He was tall and rail thin, and wore tight-ass, skinny jeans and a black holey concert T-shirt of a band I'd never heard of.

"Come on, I'll show you where the school is," Shane said, motioning for me to follow.

Milo and Richie dropped their boards and started down the street.

Shane and I walked in silence, and I hated that we felt awkward with each other. There was so much unspoken tension that I wondered if our relationship would ever recover. "Hey, I was wondering if you wanted to check out the castle after registration."

He didn't look the least bit interested.

"The family who owns it is away for the summer," I added. "It's closed to the public, so we'd have to break in. I totally understand if you don't want to."

His eyes instantly lit up. "Count me in."

Braemar High was an old brick building that smelled oddly similar to my school back home in Portland. It had three levels, and given my schedule, I knew I'd be getting a lot of exercise running up and down the stairs since my classes were scattered throughout each floor.

Shane had bailed on me shortly after arriving at the school, telling me we'd meet up later at the castle. I wasn't holding my breath, especially now that he'd found buddies, but at least we were talking. That was a good start.

Only one girl had approached me in the two hours I was at registration, and as sweet as she'd been, I knew we would never be close friends. We were just too different, and honestly, I didn't know if I could let anyone in after losing all my buddies back home. I realized I hadn't helped matters by pulling away after my mom's death, but still, it hurt that everyone had let go so easily.

And what about Ian? Did I feel it was okay to befriend him because he was a ghost? I'd never had a guy friend, well—aside from Kerry Johnston in the first grade, but that hardly counted. Playing hide-and-seek on the school playground was a lot different than a sixteen-year-old girl hanging out with a nineteen-year-old guy.

I rushed over the bridge and past the inn. I didn't spare the cemetery a glance, and even stayed on the opposite side of the road.

Before I knew it, I was at the castle's driveway, sliding under the chain.

I avoided looking over at the trees, not wanting or needing a reminder that I had cut yesterday.

"It's sort of creepy."

I jumped at the sound of Shane's voice. His hands were shoved into his jeans pockets, and his eyes were seriously bloodshot. No wonder I hadn't been able to find him after registration. He'd been getting blazed with his new friends.

"Yeah, it is," I said, not blaming him for getting high. I'd smoked pot a few times with my friend Ashley. I never did understand the appeal. I felt paranoid and awkward, and I ate anything in sight. Not pretty.

"So are you sure about this?" he asked, sounding hesitant.

Nothing short of cops showing up was going to stop me from getting inside that castle. "Yep. Are you?"

His eyes were mere slits, and the sides of his mouth curved the slightest bit. I had a feeling he wouldn't be a huge help if we ran into trouble, but at least I wouldn't be alone.

"Let's do it." He motioned for me to go ahead of him, and he followed behind as we walked into the castle's courtyard that was hidden behind a tall stone wall. As expected, the front entry door was locked, and as we rounded the back I saw painting supplies beside a partially opened window.

I glanced at Shane. "You want to try it?"

His eyes widened. "I don't know. It looks kind of small. I don't think I could squeeze through."

He could fit, but I was the one who wanted to see the castle. He was here at my invitation, and if he wanted to stay outside and play lookout, then that was fine with me.

"Whistle if anyone comes, okay?"

He nodded, looking relieved. "Okay. Be careful."

I pushed the window up, remembering when Ashley and I had sneaked out of my bedroom back home.

I dangled from the window frame for a second, and then dropped down onto the floor. The smell of paint was nearly overwhelming, and across the room there was a ladder, which would come in handy if I needed to leave in a hurry.

I walked out of the room and headed down a hallway that had black-and-white photos of landscapes, all in black frames with white matting.

I came upon a spiral staircase and my heart started racing. The first landing was the entryway where visitors were greeted by an ancient-looking sword that was taller than I was. It had been carefully displayed against a tartan, in what I assumed must be the family's colors. I hesitated, wondering what in the hell I was thinking. True, Ian had lived here hundreds of years ago, but it was someone else's home now. What if there were hidden security cameras?

Despite my misgivings, I pushed on. After all, it's not like I was here to steal anything. I just wanted to see where Ian had lived.

The first room I came to was an office. Plastic covered the bookcases, chairs, computer equipment, and desks, and the smell of paint was very strong.

The next doorway led into the dining room. I stepped inside, my heart hammering in my ears. A large table sat directly beneath a large, ornate golden chandelier. Near the fireplace were two red velvet chairs and a coffee table.

My eyes were drawn to the painting of a beautiful woman that hung above the fireplace, her resemblance to Ian unmistakable. She had the same dark hair, light blue eyes, and sensual lips. Was she his mother? It was impossible to know the age of the painting, and there was no nameplate or date to help me figure it out.

Is this where Ian died, I wondered, imagining what the space must have looked like two centuries ago. Suddenly a strange pressure started in my chest and throat. I pressed my hand to my chest and winced.

Was Ian here now?

I headed for the stairs when a cold blast of air enveloped me. I stopped in my tracks and turned just in time to see a black figure dart across the room. Startled, I bit the inside of my cheek to keep from crying out.

As the seconds ticked by, a wave of uneasiness washed over me. "Ian," I said, growing more restless by the second.

There was no answer.

I heard a loud whistle though, followed by the unmistakable sound of tires on gravel.

Shit! I rushed out of the room and down the spiral staircase. My heart thundered in my ears as I raced into the room where Shane had his face up to the window. "Hurry," he said, looking over his shoulder.

I pulled the ladder over to the window and scrambled up and out. I closed the window, leaving it open a couple of inches—just as I'd found it. Hopefully no one would be the wiser.

A car door shut and Shane put his finger to his lips. A painter, dressed in white coveralls and work boots, strode into the courtyard, whistling. We hung back while he unlocked the castle's front door and stepped inside.

After the entry door closed, we walked fast toward the entrance, out onto the lawn, keeping close to the wall, before rushing toward the trees.

A strange chill worked its way along my spine, signaling we weren't alone. A spirit was in the vicinity. I hoped it was Ian, but for some reason I didn't think it was. The presence felt dark.

"Fuckin' A, that was close," Shane said, looking back over his shoulder.

"Yeah, it was." I had to pick up my pace to keep in stride with him. "Thanks for coming with me."

"It was fun," Shane said, even though his expression said something altogether different.

We came upon the cemetery and that's when I saw her—a girl about my age, sitting on the stone wall. She was a spirit, her figure not at all solid, but transparent. I could see her well enough to make out her strange style of clothing and knew that, like Ian, she wasn't from my time.

She had long brown hair that fell in thick curls to her tiny waist. A plain green gown came to her ankles and she was barefoot. There was no expression at all on her pale face, but there was something intensely creepy about her dark eyes. I looked away, but knew with a sickening feeling I had stared too long.

My thoughts were confirmed when she followed us across the road, and into the meadow which backed to the inn.

I so didn't want her following us home.

My throat felt tight, and I found it harder to breathe.

I started choking, the tightening around my neck growing more intense by the second. Was the girl signaling to me she had died by way of strangulation?

"Are you okay?" Shane asked, and I nodded, unable to form a reply.

Miss Akin stepped outside onto the back porch, a basket of laundry propped on her hip. Seeing us, she waved.

I waved back, never so relieved to see anyone. Maybe the ghost would leave—

"*Riiileeeey*," came a chilling whisper in my ear.

The breath lodged in my throat, and when I turned, the ghost was gone.

Chapter Five

"Are you alright, my love?"

I turned to Miss Akin, who was busy kneading dough on the kitchen counter. Since returning to the house some twenty minutes before, I hadn't left her side. Honestly, I was afraid to. Not that I believed the ghost could hurt me, but she had unsettled me in a way that would make falling asleep tonight tough.

"Yeah, I'm fine," I said to pacify her. I was far from fine. I could still see the ghost, those dark eyes—that terrifying stare and the dread that had filled me when I'd noticed her sitting on the cemetery stone wall.

I glanced out the window, half expecting her to be there, staring back at me. *Would she dare come in?*

Did Ian know her? I mean, was it possible for two ghosts to exist and not be aware of the other? I chewed my bottom lip. But why would he not see her and I could?

"So, did you and your brother go to the castle?" Miss Akin asked.

My heart gave a jolt. "Yeah, I wanted Shane to see it."

"I figured that's where you must be coming from. It's lovely, isn't it?"

"I don't know if I would call it lovely, but it has elements that are," I said, and Miss Akin laughed, immediately lifting my somber mood.

"I suppose it's more formidable than beautiful, but the setting is quite unique," she said in the castle's defense.

"Do you know anything about the castle's history?"

Miss Akin nodded. "Sure, what are you curious about?"

I couldn't very well just come right out and ask about Ian or the picture of the woman hanging above the fireplace in the castle's dining room without blowing the fact that I'd broken in. "Well, it's kind of a creepy place and I'm wondering if there are any scary stories."

"You mean ghost stories?" she asked, lifting a brow.

Anticipation built within me. "Yeah."

She grabbed a rolling pin from a cabinet and went at the dough like a maniac. "Any dwelling that has been around for as long as the castle is bound to house a few ghosts. One story is about a man known as Hanway, who was the MacKinnons' most ardent enemy, and who made a large sum by stealing cattle from right beneath his victim's noses. Hanway and his sons stole upwards of forty head of cattle from Laird MacKinnon one night. A servant keeping guard saw him, shot him, and he fell from his horse. The servant brought Hanway to his master, who in turn saw to his wound, and when the man was well enough, he was promptly imprisoned in the castle dungeon."

"How long was he imprisoned for?"

"A year, I believe."

"A year? That seems like a long time for stealing a few cows."

Miss Akin snorted. "Perhaps to you it might sound like a long time for such a deed, but given the fact they used to hang people for such offenses, I say he got off lightly. However, Hanway did not take to his imprisonment very kindly, and each night everyone from miles around could hear his screams. Rumors suggest he was tortured, which I do not believe to be the case since Laird MacKinnon was known for being a fair and just ruler. Others say Hanway was slowly losing his mind, screaming for his family and loved ones. Well, one night, the screaming ceased and Laird MacKinnon checked the dungeon and found the man dead as could be, his nails ripped off and his fingertips bloodied from where he had clawed at the door. There are some who say his spirit still roams the castle, and visitors have commented on hearing a scratching sound coming from the basement, which happened to be used as the dungeon."

Thank God I hadn't seen the Hanway ghost while I was at the castle. Or maybe I had. Maybe the dark shadow in the dining room had been his spirit? "Are there any others who died at the castle?"

Miss Akin's brows furrowed. "Well, let's see, during the eighteenth century the castle laird had been killed during a bloody battle with a rival clan, and his cousin, who was living on the Isle of Skye, moved into the castle with his new wife. It is said that the woman's beauty was talked about all over Scotland. They had four children, all of whom resembled their lovely mother. The eldest boy was truly a handsome young devil, and the girls from the village and beyond took notice of him. Many believed he would marry a family friend, the daughter of a wealthy landowner named Murray, who lived in an adjoining county."

"Why didn't they marry?"

"This is where the story turns tragic. You see, there was a young servant girl who worked in the castle, along with her father, and she became enamored with the young MacKinnon."

My pulse skittered. "Do you remember his name?"

Her brow furrowed. "Let's see, there were two sons. I think the names were Ian and Duncan, and if I'm not mistaken, Ian was the eldest."

The hair on my arms stood on end. Now we were getting somewhere. Plus, for the first time ever I was getting validation about the spirits I was seeing.

"This servant girl fell desperately in love with Ian, who in turn was expected to marry someone of his own station. This would be common knowledge of the time, but this did not stop the servant from falling in love with him. So when it came to pass that the young MacKinnon began spending time with Murray's daughter, a woman who would be considered a suitable match for a laird's son, the servant became so jealous she poisoned him. Ian died right there in front of his devastated family."

"What happened to the servant?" I asked, sitting on the edge of my seat.

"The family had her hanged from a tree on the castle grounds."

I swallowed past the lump in my throat. What if the ghost I had seen had been the servant who had killed Ian? "Do you believe in ghosts, Miss Akin?" I asked, shifting in my seat as I waited for her to answer.

She watched me for a long, uncomfortable minute before responding. "Yes, I do, and I take it you do as well given your questions."

I nodded.

"Let me ease your fears, my dear. I have never heard of an instance where a ghost has harmed a human. True, they have scared a fair share of the living nearly out of their skins, but as far as doing true harm, that can never be."

I was ready to question her more when I felt a strange vibration race through me. A familiar quickening that made me aware someone was with us.

I stood up. "I just thought of something," I said. "I, uh—might need to switch a class."

"If there's anything I can help you with, let me know, my dear," Miss Akin said, but I was already heading for my room.

I opened the door to my bedroom and found Ian sprawled out on my bed, his arms pillowed behind his head. He looked entirely too comfortable, and I was absolutely ecstatic to see him.

"Make yourself at home," I said, and he turned to me, a heart-melting smile on his gorgeous face. Not taking my eyes off of him, I shut the door behind me and walked toward him, intent on finding answers.

"I did not think you would mind, Riley."

I liked when he said my name, the way he rolled the *R*. "I don't mind," I said, sitting down on the edge of the bed. I tried not to let his good looks or close proximity get in the way of the questions I had, but I couldn't ignore the sudden racing of my heart. "So...I went to the castle today."

He sat up on his elbows. "Yes, I know."

Now that surprised me. "How?"

The sides of his mouth curved in a boyish grin. "I have my ways."

I hated that I was being serious and he wasn't. I was happy he was here, but also wary that he hadn't been straight with me about the servant. "I think I saw the girl who killed you today."

He immediately dropped his gaze to my comforter and ran his hand over the material, tracing the filigree pattern with a long finger. "I didn't want you to be afraid of her."

"Have you been able to see her all this time?"

Sliding off the bed, he walked over to the window and looked out. "Yes, but Laria stays near the graveyard, away from me...and I stay away from her."

No wonder I had felt such a creepy sensation when I first saw that cemetery. "When was the last time you saw her?"

"It's difficult to say," he said, turning to face me again. "You see, time is not the same for you as it is for me."

I frowned. "What?"

"Time in the spirit world is different than time as you know it."

What did that mean, anyway? Frustrated, I ran my hands down my face. "Should I be afraid of Laria?"

"You should be wary."

"Miss Akin said ghosts can't harm the living."

I could tell by his expression that he felt differently, and that made me nervous.

"I believe Laria is as dangerous in death as she was in life," he replied. "Perhaps more so. I don't know if it's her connection to the Black Arts that makes her so powerful, but you must be careful."

Black Arts? As in witchcraft? "How much harm can she do? I mean...she's dead."

"You would do well to remember that she's the one who cursed me."

"I'm not afraid of her," I said, even though I actually was. Laria made me really nervous. And I could tell by Ian's reaction that I needed to be worried. "I wonder if there's a book about witchcraft and spells that can help end the curse?"

"It's generous of you to try and help me, but I can't ask you to put yourself in harm's way."

"I want to help you," I said, pulling off the elastic band from around my ponytail and running my fingers through my hair. Ian's eyes followed my movements, and when our gazes locked again, he smiled.

I felt that smile all the way to my toes.

Tossing the hair band on my nightstand, I blurted, "Maybe I could check the library or the Internet. I mean, my dad promised to have the computer up and running by the weekend, but I really don't want to wait that long, you know?" Oh my God, I was rambling, but I couldn't help it. The way he was looking at me made me kind of nervous, but not in a bad way. Rather, an excited, *I-can't-wait-to-see-what-happens-next* kind of way. "Maybe we can go to the library after lunch."

He nodded, but looked hesitant for some reason.

"What's wrong?" I asked, almost afraid of his answer.

"Are you sure about this, Riley? Perhaps you should think about what you are truly getting into first."

I wanted to tell him that there was absolutely no going back. "I want to help you end this curse, Ian. What Laria did to you was wrong and you deserve to have peace."

He stared at me for a long minute, saying nothing—just watching me with a soft expression that made my insides tighten.

"Thank you, Riley," he finally said. "Thank you."

Chapter Six

The town library was old and surprisingly large, but had a seriously disappointing New Age section.

A girl about my age stood behind the front counter, helping a woman and her young daughter check out books. She watched me closely as I browsed the aisles, and I wondered if checking out books on ghosts and witchcraft was a smart thing to do given how new I was. With my luck, by the time school started everyone would be talking. Oh well, it wasn't like people talking behind my back was new to me.

Ian stood beside me, his fingers brushing along the book spines. I wondered what the girl at the counter and the other patrons would think if they knew there was a ghost in their midst.

I pulled an old book off the shelf entitled *How to Hex your Lover*, and saw Ian give me a sidelong glance. When our gazes met he rolled his eyes, but a smile curved his lips.

I laughed under my breath and noticed at that exact moment an old man sitting in a nearby chair, watching me over the rim of his bifocal glasses. I hoped he didn't think I'd been laughing at him.

The man's brows furrowed as his gaze shifted back to his book.

Ian leaned against me, his shoulder touching mine as he gazed down at the page. His long hair brushed against my cheek, and I smiled at the comfortable relationship we shared. It must have been horrible to live for so long in the shadows, trying to get others to notice you, and to know that you were cursed to spend eternity as a spirit. I was resolved to help him, no matter what it took. And let's face it; focusing on someone else's problems was good for me. "Anything of interest?" he asked.

I ran a finger down the table of contents and refrained from saying the chapter headings aloud, especially with the old man and the girl behind the counter watching me so closely.

"I'll check this one out for sure," I said under my breath, and grabbed another book about ghosts off the shelf. My heart nearly leapt out of my chest when I saw a chapter heading that read, "Can ghosts see us in the shower?"

Oh hell no...

I flipped right past that particular chapter, but I could feel my cheeks turn hot. Oh my God, what if Ian *could* see me naked in the shower? I had just always assumed spirits popped in and out, with no rhyme or reason. Since I could see ghosts, then wouldn't I know when they were in turn watching me?

The problem with that theory was that I also "felt" spirits during those times they didn't manifest or show themselves. Just like when I'd felt the ugly energy right before Laria appeared. How long had she been watching me before I had seen her? What if ghosts were always around—and I just didn't see or even feel them all the time? I realized there was so much I didn't know about the spirit world, and it was really in my best interest to learn as much as I could, no matter how frightening it might be.

"Hey!"

I jumped at the voice coming from directly behind me. Ian turned. I did too.

It was the girl from the front desk. She was tiny, standing about five feet and weighing maybe a hundred pounds. She had shoulder-length curly red hair and surprisingly huge boobs. Apparently she wasn't afraid of showing cleavage, because her emerald green V-neck sweater hugged every curve. I glanced at Ian to see if he'd taken notice.

He had. His gaze was focused on the girl's D cups. Typical male...

It was all I could do not to elbow him in the gut. "Hey," I said, shifting on my feet, aware of the book in my hand.

"My name's Megan. You just moved into the old inn, right?"

"Yeah, I did." I extended my free hand. "I'm Riley."

"Nice to meet you, Riley." She had a firm handshake for someone so small. "I didn't see you at registration this morning, but I heard about you."

Oh great. I wondered what exactly she'd heard.

"I met your brother. He's coming by my boyfriend Milo's house tonight. Would you like to come?"

Shane hadn't mentioned anything about a party, so I had to wonder if he wanted me tagging along.

I looked over at Ian, wondering what he thought.

"She cannot see me, Riley," he said, sitting on a nearby table. "You keep lookin' away and she will think you are rude...or a bit soft in the head." He said this last with a wink, and I returned my attention to Megan.

"Sure, I'd love to come," I said, and Megan grinned, looking genuinely happy that I'd accepted.

"Excellent. I already gave your brother directions. So, we'll see you at around eight o'clock?"

"Sure."

"Okay then." She glanced at the book in my hand. "Do you want to check that out?"

"Yeah, but I'm going to look at a few more first, and maybe browse the Internet while I'm at it."

"We only have one computer," she said apologetically, pointing toward the back corner of the library where a middle-school-aged girl typed furiously on the keys. "Alice Pengres is on it yet again." She rolled her eyes. "I wish her parents would get Internet service already. She's here every bloody day for hours on end. I swear she clocks more time here than I do."

I shrugged. "Oh well, I'll just have to wait until we get Internet service at my house. My dad promised we'd have a connection by this weekend."

"Well, I'll warn you right now that the speed is a bit dodgy in this town. Some days you get on fast, and some days it's as slow as can be."

Since my dad was a software designer, he used the best of the best when it came to technology, so Internet speed usually wasn't a problem, but then again we weren't in Portland anymore. "Well, I'd better get back to searching."

"And I'd better get back to work before Mrs. Landridge returns from break."

"I'll see you tonight," I said, and as she walked away, I glanced over at Ian and was surprised he was looking at me and not Megan.

"See, you are making friends already," he said, sounding happy for me.

"Looks that way," I said, excited I'd been invited to Milo's. I just hoped Shane wouldn't be pissed I was going.

The old man cleared his throat loudly, and Ian smiled and took hold of my hand. "Come on, we had better get out of here."

Chapter Seven

I tried to calm my nerves as I walked with Shane up the cobblestone pathway leading to Milo's house. The last time I'd been to a party had been the night before the accident that killed my mom. It felt strange, and somehow wrong—and the only thing that kept me walking toward the door was the fact I wanted to spend time with Shane.

Speaking of Shane, he actually had looked relieved when I told him I was going to the party. Aside from our trip to the castle, I tried to recall the last time we hung out together. We used to attend dances at a gym called "Hoops" where we'd dance all night with our friends to bad techno music. Back then we'd always got along, and always defended each other if the other one was in trouble of any kind...that was until I started hanging out with Ashley.

Meeting Ashley had been the beginning of the end for me. I thought she was so cool, so different from Becca and my other friends. I was a dancer, on the honor roll, and I didn't smoke, drink, or do drugs, but Ashley did. And she convinced me that my life would be so much better if I did too.

In my starry-eyed mode, I'd turned away from everything I had known, including my family. And then Shane had started acting out and my parents had blamed me, which in turn made me push them even farther away.

Music blared through the open windows of the gray stone cottage that had a gingerbread house look about it. My heart picked up speed with every step that brought us closer. I had spent an hour getting ready and hoped I wasn't overdressed. I'd opted for a black button-down shirt and dark jeans with a pair of wedge heels. For the first time in months, I had curled my hair and put on makeup. As I'd been getting ready, I couldn't help but wonder what Ian would think of the outfit, or how I looked.

Shane knocked on the door. A second later the door flew open and Milo was there, smiling from ear to ear. "Welcome, American friends," he said with a terrible American accent.

His gaze caught mine and he whistled through his teeth as he looked me up and down.

"Dude, seriously," Shane said, sounding irritated.

I had to admit Shane's behavior surprised me in a good way. I liked knowing he had my back.

Milo threw up his hands. "Dude, I'm just saying big sister's smokin' hot." The words sounded strange with his Scottish accent, but his effort to come off as American made me smile. The compliment didn't hurt either.

Milo gestured for us to enter.

"Thanks," I said, slipping past him, anxiously looking around the room at the others who stared back at us. Uncomfortable, I shifted on my feet.

Aside from the pounding music, the voices had quieted, and as Milo shut the door, I fought the urge to turn and run, back to the safety of my room and Ian.

I finally relaxed when I saw Megan come toward me. She had a drink in one hand, and when our eyes met, I could tell it wasn't her first.

She grinned. "Hey, I was wondering if you were gonna show." She gave me a big hug and spilled some of her drink on my sleeve and the rest onto the floor.

"Thanks for inviting me," I said, grabbing on to a nearby chair to keep from falling over with her on top of me.

"Watch it, love," Milo said, righting the glass and pulling Megan toward him. "My mum will have my head if I make a mess of the place."

Megan snorted. "Yeah, your mum will be livid once she learns you had a party while she was away." I could tell she struggled to focus. If she drank much more, she'd be on her ass in no time.

I looked around the room and saw Shane was already busy tossing back a straight shot. A small crowd had rallied around him and they roared their approval.

At the front of the crowd was a younger girl with black hair, multiple piercings, and black, emo-style clothing. She appeared to have her eye on Shane, and I had the feeling he had noticed her too, from the way he watched her.

My little brother was definitely growing up.

"You want a drink?" Megan asked.

"I don't know," I said, and both Milo and Megan groaned. I had no desire to get drunk in front of strangers. My dad had always said you only had one shot at making a first impression.

Megan's lower lip jutted out. "Come on, Riley. Don't be a buzzkill."

Buzzkill Riley—not a nickname I was wanting.

"Sure, why not." I was determined to sip on the drink in case

Shane might need my help walking home later. One of us had to be clear-headed when we faced our dad, who'd been surprisingly chatty at dinner. Both Shane and I had contributed little to the conversation, other than nod and answer each of his mundane questions. He seemed to like his job, which was good, but it also meant any chance of moving back to Portland wasn't going to happen anytime soon.

"And you must be Riley," said a gorgeous guy with light brown eyes and shaggy brown hair. He had an athletic body, and wore a button-down blue-and-white-striped shirt, dark jeans, and skater shoes that he hadn't bothered to lace. Aside from the unlaced shoes, he seemed fashionable and was definitely a hottie...and every girl in the vicinity seemed to notice him.

"Yeah, that's me."

"I'm Johan," he said, shaking my hand.

"An original name."

He flashed a grin, and my heart actually skipped a beat. "My parents would like to think so."

Milo pushed a drink into my hand. "Drink up, Riley," he said, waiting for me to do just that.

I brought the neon green plastic glass to my lips and winced as the strong liquor burned my mouth.

Two girls came up to me and introduced themselves, but I quickly got the feeling they were using me to get to Johan, since they kept throwing glances his way. To his credit, he seemed oblivious to all the attention.

I listened to the conversation going on all around me, while keeping an eye on Shane. I felt uneasy when he took yet another straight shot. I didn't want to go off on him like our dad would if he knew Shane was drinking, but I didn't want him getting sloppy drunk in front of people he'd just met either.

"He'll be okay," Johan said.

I smiled. "That obvious, huh?"

"It's good you're looking out for him. That's what family is for."

I nodded. I seriously wondered what others would think of my family if they knew the truth, especially about me. A girl who could see and talk to ghosts wasn't exactly the norm. And God forbid they found out about my cutting. Back home I'd managed to keep my secret relatively safe, but I'd also become a loner in the process.

"I have a confession to make," he said, and I instantly straightened, afraid of his next words. "I saw you today at registration and tried to get your attention."

I sighed inwardly. "I'm sorry, I didn't see you."

"Yeah, you seemed a bit preoccupied." He leaned into me, his lips close to my ear. "How about I introduce you around?" His breath was hot against my neck and I couldn't ignore the sudden racing of my heart.

"Sure," I said, following behind him. Johan stayed by my side every second, except when I excused myself and went to the bathroom, where I poured the mixed drink into the sink, and set the cup on the cluttered kitchen counter on my way back to the living room.

Unfortunately, when I returned, I noticed Shane was getting really clumsy, nearly knocking over an end table and lamp.

We would have to leave soon, and I knew he'd probably argue with me, but I wasn't leaving without him. I'd pull in reinforcements if I had to, although I was beginning to think I might be the only sober person in the place.

Johan put his hand on my hip. "Come on, loosen up, big sister."

Granted, the attention was nice...but he was getting a little too comfortable, and I didn't want anyone getting certain ideas. "We need to go soon. Our dad is pretty strict."

He nodded in understanding, though he looked disappointed that I was going to leave. "I'll walk you home, if you'd like."

"Thanks," I said, grateful for the offer. Shane was going to be a handful, and I could use all the help I could get. "Maybe in about twenty minutes?"

"Sounds good," he said, flashing a smoldering smile that made me feel slightly flushed.

The warm and fuzzy feeling left me when from the corner of my eye I saw someone watching me. Uneasiness rippled along my spine, and when I turned, I noticed a girl staring at me from across the room.

My stomach fell to my toes.

Laria.

She moved behind a group of people. She wasn't walking, but rather *gliding* across the floor, moving in exaggerated slow motion. Every time I caught a glimpse of her, those dark eyes were looking straight at me and I swear she never blinked.

I stepped closer to Johan and didn't even realize that I'd reached for his hand until his fingers threaded through mine. Terrified, I squeezed his hand as Laria stopped beside Shane.

Warning bells rang in my ears when Laria put a hand on Shane's shoulder. She turned her face toward the side of his, her lips near his ear, and she whispered something, all the while she watched me.

Shane, who had been talking to Richie, stopped in mid-sentence, his brows furrowing as he looked to his right. Richie just kept on talking, but I could see the disturbed look in my brother's eyes. He leaned forward, set his drink on the table, and shook his head as though to clear it.

The corners of Laria's mouth curved in a malicious smile as her hand slid toward Shane's neck, her fingers squeezing tight—

Shane started coughing, and I rushed over to him, reached out, and jerked him toward me.

"Let's go," I said louder than necessary, my gaze shifting to Laria, who laughed maliciously, the sound making the hair on my arms stand on end.

My cheeks burned as the others looked at me like I'd lost my mind. I was probably coming off as a bitch, but there's not much I could do about it.

Thank God Shane didn't argue with me. He brushed his hand over his neck—in the exact spot Laria's hand had been moments before.

Johan was beside me a second later, his hand resting at my back. "Is everything okay?"

"Yeah, I think it's just time for us to leave. Will you walk us home now?"

He nodded, still looking surprised by my strange behavior. "Sure, no problem."

"Thanks again," I said, relieved to have him with me. I was terrified out of my mind, and the last thing I wanted was to face Laria alone, with only my wasted brother to protect me.

I glanced at Laria and her head tilted to the side at a strange, impossible angle, a twisted smile on her lips. I could hear bones cracking.

She was trying to freak me out, and she was doing a damn good job of it.

"*Riiiiiley—Riiiiiley—Riiiiiley—Riiiiiley...*" She said my name over and over again.

Her sinister laughter rang out, and then her expression changed abruptly as her gaze jerked to something—or someone—directly behind me. She took a step back, then another, her expression a mixture of fear and anger.

My pulse skittered as I looked over my shoulder.

Ian.

I don't think I've ever been so relieved to see someone.

Laria glanced at me, ran a finger across her throat, and then shot to the ceiling...and was gone.

Ian's expression was intense, his eyes fierce, and his form more translucent than I'd ever before seen. Appearing to me had to be taking a toll on him, and yet he had come here to protect me.

"Who's Ian?" Johan asked.

"A friend," I said absently. I hadn't even realized I'd said his name aloud.

I wanted to go to Ian and hug him tight, but as I walked toward him, he began to fade before my eyes.

I opened my mouth to say something—anything—but in a flash, he was gone.

Chapter Eight

The morning passed without any sign of Ian, and I was beginning to worry that Laria had done something to him. But what could one ghost do to another? I mean, technically they were both already dead, so how could she hurt him?

Ian had told me Laria was powerful and dangerous. Now I was beginning to understand just how dangerous. Look at the way she had whispered in Shane's ear at Milo's party, at the way she had squeezed his neck, and he'd felt it, because he'd started choking.

Had I inadvertently put my family in danger because of my friendship with Ian?

Desperate for information on ghosts and spells, I reached for the library books I'd stashed in my nightstand. I had already scoured the book on witches and spells, and came up with very little information that would help me in Ian's case—except about standard love and hate spells. One love spell said to make a doll out of clay, wax, or by sewing a straw figure of the person you longed for, carving their name in your blood on said doll's chest, sticking a pin in its heart, and reciting a phrase each night of a full moon. If you did all those things, then the person you desired would fall madly in love with you...or so the book said.

That last bit made me smirk. *Yeah, right*, I thought, but the more I read, the more I wondered if any of these strange rituals worked. I knew that witches still existed, and even had their own religion. But did they have actual powers—like the ability to cast spells and bind people to them?

I reminded myself that anything was possible. After all, a little over a year ago I didn't believe in ghosts.

I grabbed the book on ghosts and scanned the pages about the different types of spirits that existed, both benevolent and malevolent. Basically good and evil.

Like Ian and Laria.

It also said it took a lot of energy for ghosts to manifest and communicate with the living. Apparently the spirit used as many energy sources as they could to reveal themselves—turning lights, televisions, and radios off and on, moving items around, and even throwing things at times.

All those things scared me, but what frightened me more than anything was the thought that ghosts could tap into our thoughts, and yes, they could also see us naked.

Oh.

My.

God.

Ian could see me naked.

And he could read my mind, too.

Talk about an unfair advantage! All the less than innocent thoughts I'd had about Ian raced through my mind. Knowing he

had been able to tap into my thoughts was downright humiliating...
kind of like someone getting hold of your diary and reading your
most personal thoughts, but worse.

Maybe there was something on the Internet that would contra-
dict what the book said. After all, this could be just one person's
opinion. That didn't make it true.

Hoping I was right, I headed downstairs to my dad's study where
the only computer in the house was located. My parents had never
allowed us to have computers in our bedrooms, and I suppose I understood why, but I hated when my mom or dad would appear out
of nowhere and look over my shoulder.

Shane had gone to check out a skateboard park in a nearby town
with Milo and Richie, and my dad was at work (shocker), so I at
least had some privacy. The last time I'd seen Miss Akin she was in
the kitchen making cookies, and said something about walking to
the post office to pick up the mail.

With the coast clear, I walked into my dad's study. I liked all the
dark reddish-colored wood and the bookcases that took up an entire
wall. I ignored the pictures on the fireplace mantel though, especially the one of our family at Disneyland. It was taken two years before
the accident, when I was still dancing with my troupe, back when I
was the perfect child and my parents were so proud of me.

Pushing the bittersweet memory away, I sat down in my dad's
chair. I logged on to the Internet and waited a good twenty seconds
before Google's home page loaded. "Not too bad," I said, surprised it
hadn't taken longer, given we lived in the sticks.

I typed the word "curses" into the search engine and a ton of cuss
words came up. I laughed and typed in "spells and curses," and up
popped a multitude of websites on witches and magic.

The first fifteen minutes I spent browsing forums where people asked basic witchcraft questions. The majority of the responses were from skeptics who told the writer of the post to find God.

Thirty minutes into my search I found an interesting website that talked about generational hexes, where one member of a family would be cursed, which in turn would curse the rest of the family. One well-known English lord had found a family living in one of his homes without paying rent. He threw the impoverished family out of the place and the old woman, a witch apparently, cursed the man and his family. Soon after the man's eldest son died, followed by another, until four of his six children were dead. The man had been crushed by a horse and killed within the fifth year, and it said that the curse died with him.

But a generational curse wasn't Ian's problem. Ian had been cursed at the time of his death.

I continued searching, and my heart leapt when I found a link about Black Magic death spells. That's when I heard footsteps sound from behind me.

Shit! Had my dad come home already?

I couldn't say I was doing research for a school assignment since school hadn't started yet.

I slowly turned.

"Sorry to disturb you, my dear, but I thought you might like a cookie and a tall glass of milk," Miss Akin said, setting a plate of shortbread cookies on the top of my dad's polished mahogany desk.

I breathed a sigh of relief, thankful it wasn't my dad. "Thanks, Miss A."

She smiled, and her gaze skipped to the computer screen. Her grin faded fast. "Is there someone who is giving you trouble?"

I cleared my throat. "No..."

"Do you mind?" she asked, nodding toward the chair on the opposite side of the desk.

I shook my head, dreading her next words. I could see it now. She'd corner my dad the minute he hit the front door, and tell him I was googling Black Magic and asking her about ghosts. He would call my shrink, who would then prescribe those pills that made me numb and sleep all day.

She took a seat and smoothed her hands over the well-worn apron. "Does your curiosity stem from the questions you asked me the other day...about the castle's history. About the ghosts?"

I sat up straighter, reached for a cookie, and killed time by taking a bite. I considered lying, but had a feeling she could read me too well for that. Plus, I had never been a good liar. Not to mention guilt would eat at me and it just wasn't worth it.

"Don't worry, love. I won't say a word to anyone, nor will I judge you."

I'd heard that one before. "You'll think I'm crazy."

"No, I won't," she said matter-of-factly, and oddly enough I believed her.

But how much did I tell her? Should I come clean about being able to see Ian and Laria's spirits, or should I just say I was intrigued by the stories she'd told me about the castle ghosts and had decided to do a little investigating of my own?

She stared at me patiently, awaiting an answer.

The cookie stuck in my throat, and I reached for the milk, took a drink, and set the glass back down. Was I ready to tell someone I could see spirits and open up that door? Miss Akin seemed like an awesome lady, but what if she thought I was crazy?

I debated just how much to reveal to her. "You know the story you told me about Laird MacKinnon's oldest son who was killed by the servant back in the eighteenth century?"

"Yes."

My heart pounded in my ears. "What if I told you I believed he was cursed by the girl who killed him, and he can't move on—as in, pass over to the other side."

"Cursed," she said, calm as could be, but her throat contracted as she swallowed hard.

"That's right. He can't leave here...ever."

"What makes you believe such is the case? Did you read something on the Internet?"

I straightened my shoulders, cleared my throat. "Because...he told me so himself."

I waited for it...the wide eyes, the fear in her face, the *I-need-to-find-another-job-immediately* expression. "When did he tell you this, dear?"

"He appeared to me the day I arrived in Braemar. In fact, the minute I stepped foot in the inn he was here." I swallowed hard, and then blurted, "Miss Akin, I can see ghosts."

Her gaze shifted over my face, and then suddenly, the sides of her mouth curved upward and she clapped her hands together. "I thought you were a sensitive, my dear. I wondered why you looked so frightened when you came home from the castle that day. When you asked me so many questions, I assumed that you had seen one of the castle ghosts."

I was so relieved she didn't think I was crazy. "So you believe me?"

"Of course I believe you. If you say you can see the spirits, then it must be true. There are people who are blessed with such gifts. Anne Marie, who is my best friend, is one. You would not have been given such abilities if you were not meant to use them, love. I have intuitive abilities myself, and have even had a few precognitive dreams, but I cannot see the dead like you can. I wish I could."

She wished she could see ghosts? Seriously? I never thought any-one would *want* to see the dead and actually look upon it as a gift. I hadn't expected such a non-judgmental reaction. "What is a precogni-tive dream?"

"It's when you dream about an event before it happens. Many people have such a gift, but they pass it off as coincidence." She leaned forward. "But enough about me. I want to know—do you mean to help the MacKinnon lad?"

"Yes, Ian needs me, but I don't know how to help him. I went to the library and checked out books on witches, spells, and ghosts, and aside from a few random spells, there was nothing about lifting a spe-cific curse someone else has made."

She tapped her fingers on the chair's armrest. "I will have to speak to Anne Marie. She may be able to help you in this matter."

I was excited at the prospect of meeting Anne Marie. "I wonder if she's seen Laria or Ian before?"

"She has never mentioned either of them, but that is certainly something you can ask her when you meet. I'll call her to see when a good time to visit would be."

"Thank you, Miss Akin."

"You're welcome, love. We'll find some answers for you both. In the meantime, you eat those cookies. You're much too thin. We need to plump you up a bit. Put some meat on those bones." She stood, smoothed her hands over her apron, and then stopped. "Tell me this...is the MacKinnon boy as handsome as history makes him out to be?"

I couldn't help but grin. Handsome didn't even begin to describe Ian. If he were alive today, he'd be the hottest guy in town...or maybe all of Scotland, but I didn't tell Miss Akin that. Instead, I nodded.

She gave a long, drawn-out sigh. "Lucky girl."

Chapter Nine

I stared out the car window, frustrated and angry that my mom had trapped me inside her Mercedes instead of finding a neutral zone in our house to talk.

And all because I'd been out after curfew and didn't call. Big, freakin' deal. I'd made it home, hadn't I?

Things between us had been really bad lately. It's not that she had done anything in particular. She just irritated me with her constant bitching. "Pick up your room. Put your clothes away. Empty the dishwasher." Why did she care if my room was picked up or my bed was made, anyway? It's not like anyone else had to see it, and I kept the door closed twenty-four/seven.

My mom cleared her throat. "Do you want to start...or should I?"

I sighed heavily, my breath fogging up the car window. I resisted the urge to draw a smiley face on the glass, knowing it would only piss her off more than she already was.

Feeling her eyes burning into the back of my skull, I turned and looked at her. "What do you want me to say?"

"Maybe start with why you didn't call."

I shrugged. "Time just got away from me."

Her nostrils flared. "Riley, you didn't get home until two in the morning, and when you did, you stumbled in smelling like alcohol and told me to leave you alone. You're a child and I'm your mother, and rules are in place for a reason."

I rolled my eyes.

"Don't roll your eyes at me, young lady."

"I was out with my friends and I forgot about the time."

"You're only fifteen, Riley. Much too young to be going to parties and drinking, and doing Lord knows what else. What has happened to you? Where is my daughter from a year ago? Scratch that, where is my daughter from six months ago?"

She was furious. I could tell by the way the nerve in her jaw jumped, and how her fingers tightened around the steering wheel until her knuckles turned white.

"All my friends are allowed to go to parties."

"I find that hard to believe."

"So now you're calling me a liar?"

She pressed her lips together until they disappeared into a thin line. Her chest rose and fell heavily. "I'm saying I find it hard to believe that any responsible parent would allow their fifteen-year-old daughter to party into the wee hours of the morning. I don't even know who drove you home last night, Riley. It certainly wasn't a parent."

"It was Mitch, Sarah's brother."

She relaxed a little. "Well, I just hope he wasn't drinking."

Actually, he hadn't been drinking since he had baseball practice in the morning, but I didn't tell her that because she wouldn't believe me anyway.

She never believed me.

"What kind of an example are you setting for your brother? He *looks up to you, Riley. When he sees you acting out, then he starts acting out too."*

Shane was the perfect child. He was every parent's dream—a good student and a star athlete. "Shane would never disappoint you."

Having heard the sarcasm in my voice, she shook her head. "You aren't a disappointment to me, Riley, but your father and I are concerned. Your grades are slipping and ever since you started hanging out with Ashley—"

"It's not Ashley's fault."

"Well, then why the sudden change?"

I had always been the "good" kid. I got good grades, I did everything my parents told me to do...and I'd felt invisible. I was going through the motions, but when I met Ashley, all that changed. She was different—a year older and exciting, and for whatever reason she liked me. She dressed differently, talked differently, and had hippie parents that let her do whatever she wanted. I liked hanging out with her, and I liked the attention I was getting, especially from guys. It felt good to be recognized—to not just be another face in the crowd.

"See, you don't even know the answer to that question."

"Can we just go home?" I asked.

"No, not until we get to the bottom of this. We've resolved nothing."

"What do you want me to say?"

"I don't know, Riley." Her voice became higher by the second. "All I know is that I feel like I've been living with a stranger these past months. I can't get through to you. You won't even talk to me most days."

I hated how sad she sounded.

"I miss my daughter," she said so softly, I barely heard her. But I heard her. Loud and clear.

She breathed deeply, and I could tell she was struggling to remain calm. "I have no choice but to ground you for a month."

"What?" I'd never been grounded a day in my life, ever—but the thought of being grounded for a month seemed like an eternity. I could envision Ashley and the others going on with their lives, partying, while I sat in my room night after endless night doing absolutely nothing.

I crossed my arms, furious.

"This hurts me more than it hurts you."

"Bullshit."

She gasped and looked at me with shock. I'd never cussed in front of her before.

That's when I saw the van pull out in front of us. We were going too fast. I froze, a cry of warning stuck in my throat. My mom saw my reaction though...but it was too late. The front of the car clipped the van's back bumper and sent our car swerving toward a huge oak tree.

I came awake with a start, my heart racing, sweat pouring off my forehead as I stared at the red neon numbers that read three thirty-three on my clock radio. I ran my hands down my face.

I hadn't had that dream for weeks, and had hoped I never would again. It was like ripping off a scab that had already healed—a horrible reminder of the worst day of my life.

If only I could go back and change what had happened. Why had I been such a pain in the ass? Had I just come home by curfew that night, then my mom would be here now and my life would be so different. Shane's and my dad's lives would be different. But I had taken her away from us. It was my fault she was dead, and I would never forget that.

"Riley, are you alright?" Ian asked in a gentle voice. He sat in the chair next to the window.

I released the breath I hadn't realized I'd been holding and nodded. "Yeah, I just had a bad dream."

"About your mother?"

My stomach clenched. "How did you know?"

"You called out to her in your sleep."

"You were watching me sleep?"

He motioned to the bed. "May I sit beside you for a little while?"

"Yeah, sure. I could use the company."

He sat on the edge of my bed. "Your mother's death is not your fault, Riley."

"But it was my fault," I said, blinking back tears. It was a reality I lived with day in and day out. Why else could I suddenly see dead people? Maybe like Ian, I had been cursed.

He reached out, his hand resting on my shoulder. "Yer mother died as she was supposed to. Fate decided that. Not you."

I'd spent months listening to counselors and teachers tell me the same thing, but no one could convince me differently. I knew the truth, and my mom knew the truth.

Tears ran down my face, and he wiped them away with his thumb. "It's alright," he whispered, pulling me into his arms.

Didn't he know it would never be alright? There was nothing I could ever do or say to bring my mom back. My arms slid around his neck and I rested my cheek against his wide chest. His hand moved up and down my back in a soothing gesture. He smelled like a mixture of the outdoors and a rich, spicy scent I knew I would never forget. I couldn't remember the last time I had hugged anyone like this, with such desperation, and oddly enough, I didn't want to let go. I took the comfort he offered and savored the feel of his strong arms embracing me.

Chapter Ten

Anne Marie wasn't at all what I expected. Being Miss Akin's friend, I had known she would be on the older side, but she looked ancient, her skin like wrinkled leather. Her whitish-purple hair resembled a beehive, and she was taller and on the slim side. Polyester elastic waistband pants rode high on her waist, and her white button-down shirt had been ironed to perfection. As she stared at me, she carefully removed her navy windbreaker and set it over the back of a chair.

"Would you mind if we closed the drapes?" Anne Marie asked, setting a single white candle on the card table. I had read about using candles when summoning spirits—how ghosts were drawn to the soft light.

Miss Akin nodded. "Not at all, dear." She hopped up from her chair beside the fireplace and closed the drapes.

"Should I lock the front door?" I asked, knowing we'd all be in deep shit if my dad walked through the door to find us having a séance.

"I already did, my darling," Miss Akin said, sitting back down.

I was glad Shane was with Milo, and I hoped he stayed away. I'd be horrified if he walked in right now.

Anne Marie lit the candle and sat down. She took a deep breath and released it slowly. "Let's hold hands and close our eyes," she prompted.

I did as she asked, taking both Miss Akin's and Anne Marie's hands within my own.

I felt ridiculous.

"We ask that if there are any spirits who wish to contact us, do so now," Anne Marie said in an authoritative voice. "Use our energy and let us know you are here by making a noise—be it a tap or a knock of some type."

Anne Marie breathed deeply at least a half dozen times, and I opened an eye to make sure she was okay. She seemed to be, so I closed my eye again.

"I sense a spirit with us," she said, sounding pleased.

That didn't take long. I bit the inside of my lower lip to keep from cracking a smile. Honestly, I didn't feel any spirit with us. I was skeptical. But it's not like she was getting paid for this, and what would she have to gain?

"My chest hurts something fierce," Anne Marie said, her voice weaker than before. "And my head aches a bit." She breathed deeply again. "Ah, she says her name begins with an *R*."

My pulse skittered. My mom's name was Rochelle, and she'd had head and chest trauma.

"Was it a car wreck?" Anne Marie said to no one in particular.

Now she was going too far. I abruptly pulled my hands away. "Did you see my dream from the other night? Are you reading me instead of reading a spirit?"

Anne Marie looked at me like I had punched her. "I don't know anything about your dream, dear," Anne Marie said matter-of-factly. "I know nothing about you...aside from the fact you are a fellow sensitive. Please trust me."

Miss Akin nodded and took hold of my other hand, squeezing it. "It's okay, Riley. We are here to help you, not harm you. Perhaps she can give you some of the answers you are looking for."

She was right. Anne Marie could give me answers. Plus, I had waited to hear from my mother for over a year now and this could be my only opportunity.

I closed my eyes and took a deep breath.

"She's handing me a red rose, which means she loves you."

My throat tightened and I began to tremble. I wanted to tell her I loved her too, but I couldn't push the words past my lips.

"Her energy is fading fast. She just wants you to know she's okay, Riley."

Is she mad at me? Does she blame me? Does she hate me? A hundred questions raced through my mind, but I couldn't say the words. Not in front of Miss Akin and Anne Marie. I didn't want them to know I had caused my mother's death, even if I had lived with that guilt every day since the accident.

"Are there any other spirits who would like to contact us?" Anne Marie said.

Mom, I want to talk to you. Don't leave so soon.

I was desperate to keep her here. The hair on my arms stood on end as the temperature abruptly dropped. I wanted it to be Ian, but the energy felt different from his. Darker.

I didn't bother keeping my eyes closed. In fact, I couldn't. I was too nervous.

"Her name begins with an *L*," Anne Marie said, her breath coming out in a fog.

It was all I could do to hold on to Anne Marie's hand. She felt freezing cold to the touch. "My neck hurts something fierce," she said, her brows furrowed. "My throat feels tight, like I can't breathe."

I glanced at Miss Akin, whose eyes were wide open now. She tried to give me a reassuring smile but it came off more as a grimace.

"Do you hear that?" Anne Marie asked, her eyes opening as well.

"I don't hear anything," I said, a sense of foreboding coming over me. "I just sense a dark presence."

"She's saying something over and over again," Anne Marie said. "I'm havin' a hard time making out the word."

My heart roared in my ears. Anne Marie looked at me abruptly. "I think she's saying your name, Riley. Yes, that's it. Do you know a young woman in spirit whose name begins with an *L*?"

I nodded, afraid of what was coming. "What does she want?"

"Why are you here?" Anne Marie asked.

The table lifted a few inches off the floor and fell back down with a clatter.

Miss Akin gasped, and we all dropped hands.

A knock sounded from the front door, and then on the wall right behind Miss Akin. Knocking started on every wall, coming from all over the house at once.

"Sweet Jesus," Miss Akin said, her eyes wide with fear. I had the feeling she had gotten a lot more than she'd expected. I wanted to tell her that she hadn't seen anything yet, but I didn't want to scare her.

Anne Marie jerked—and then she looked at me and didn't so much as blink. "Do not help him."

It didn't sound like Anne Marie's voice at all, but a much younger voice. Someone my age. My throat tightened. Could it be Laria? I wondered with a sick feeling.

Miss Akin must have caught the voice thingy too, because she scooted closer to me. "What do you mean, Anne Marie?"

Anne Marie turned to Miss Akin and her head tilted. She continued to just stare and Miss Akin gasped, "Anne Marie?"

The corners of Anne Marie's mouth lifted in a creepy smile before she turned back to me. "Forget him, Riley...or else."

The candle blew out and the curtains ripped open by themselves. Miss Akin let out a startled scream and put a hand to her chest. "Bloody hell—I don't think I'll be doin' that again anytime soon."

Anne Marie blinked a few times, looked at me, and then at Miss Akin. "What happened?"

Oh my God...was she serious?

"You don't remember?" I asked.

Anne Marie shook her head, glancing at Miss Akin. "I think I need to go home and rest, dear. I'm completely knackered out and my head hurts somethin' fierce."

Miss Akin had a concerned expression on her face, but she nodded. "Yes, that might be for the best. I'll see you home."

"Don't be silly. I'll be just fine. It's nothing a little nap won't cure," Anne Marie said with a reassuring smile.

"Are you sure?" I asked, following behind as she and Miss Akin walked slowly toward the front door. I felt someone in back of me—totally in my personal space, and I turned...only to find the room empty.

I didn't like feeling at such a disadvantage.

"I'll call you later," Anne Marie said, before shutting the door behind her.

Miss Akin turned and looked at me, eyes wide. "I'm so sorry, my dear. I honestly had no idea things would turn out in such a way. I thought perhaps she'd ask a few questions, but I would have never—"

Someone pounded on the door and we both jumped and let out startled gasps. "Goodness me, I don't think my heart can take much more of this," Miss Akin said before she whipped open the door.

Staring back at us was Shane, a strange expression on his face. "Why was the door locked?"

"Oh, I'm sorry about that, my darling," Miss Akin said, fidgeting with the doorknob. "I must have locked it by accident when my friend left."

"Yeah, I saw her. I think she left skid marks in the driveway."

I didn't doubt it.

Miss Akin cleared her throat. "Would you like some lunch?"

"Sure," Shane said, glancing into the parlor. "It smells like smoke in here."

"I lit a candle," I blurted, and Miss Akin took the opportunity to head for the kitchen.

There was a part of me that wanted to tell him that our mom had come through, but chances were he'd think I was crazy. Plus, I didn't want to chance it. What if Anne Marie had done her homework to begin with, and what about Laria? How could she have made all those knocks and sounds throughout the house? And what about the voice that had come out of Anne Marie? It had seemed so real, and what she had said about not helping *him*. She had to be talking about Ian.

It was just all too much to absorb.

Shane ran a hand through his hair as he walked toward the stair-case. He was on the first step when he turned to me. "Did you have a friend over last night?"

I shook my head. "No...why?"

"I could have sworn I heard you talking to someone."

My heart skipped a beat. He had obviously heard me speaking with Ian. "Maybe I was talking in my sleep."

"No...it was like a full-on conversation," he said adamantly. "You were talking to someone just like we are right now."

I swallowed hard. I had spent too many months with people thinking I was mental, my own family included. "I didn't have anyone over, so I must have talked in my sleep."

He opened his mouth, ready to argue, but I darted past him and ran upstairs. "See you at dinner."

Chapter Eleven

Ian grabbed my hand, his fingers sliding over and through mine. His touch felt incredible, sending a jolt of exhilaration up my spine.

"I want to show you something, Riley." His smile made me feel all wobbly inside, and my heart thudded against my chest as we walked across a meadow, the scent of heather so strong.

"Where are we going?" I asked, elated to be with him again.

His lips curved. "It's a surprise."

We started walking up a hill, and then Ian started to run, his laughter contagious.

"Come on, you are lagging behind." His grip on my hand tightened. "We're almost there."

The wind became stronger the higher we climbed, the trees whipping with the force. I could see we approached the top of the hill and what appeared to be a sudden drop-off. He must have sensed my hesitation to continue, because he stopped and grinned. "I wanted you to see this."

"See what?"

"Close your eyes."

I closed my eyes, trusting him completely.

He turned me so my back was to him, his hands resting on my shoulders, his breath hot against my neck. I liked the feel of his body against mine, so close, and it was all I could do not to turn in his arms and hug him tight.

"Open your eyes, Riley."

I opened my eyes and my pulse skittered. Below me I could see the entire village, the school, the inn, the cemetery, and the castle. I couldn't believe the incredible view, stretching as far as the eye could see. Green grass, trees, the river that curved through the small town. "It's breathtaking."

He nodded. "I can spend hours up here."

I didn't blame him. It was a place you could go to be alone...to think, to put things in perspective.

"This is my home, Riley. My prison."

I glanced back at him and my stomach turned seeing the pain in his eyes.

"This is where I am to spend all eternity...and I can no longer bear it."

His hands dropped from my shoulders, and he turned and walked toward the ledge.

"Ian—"

He stared at me, and then stepped off.

I sat up in bed, my heart racing.

"It was just a dream," I said to myself, reaching for the glass of water on the nightstand. The dream had seemed so real, but thank God it hadn't been. I didn't want Ian to go away—not when he had been the first person I could talk to in what seemed like forever.

I turned on my bedside lamp.

"You called out my name."

I nearly dropped the glass. Ian had to stop doing that. Granted, it was nice knowing he was around when I needed him, but seriously... "Yeah, I had another dream."

He grinned, that irresistible smile that made my insides all fluttery. "You dreamt about me?" His voice held an arrogant edge that had me rolling my eyes.

"Yes, and you jumped off a cliff."

He placed a long-fingered hand flat against his chest. "Ouch, lass."

His brilliant blue eyes held a warmth that made my toes curl. No one had looked at me in that way since Katie Jones's thirteenth birthday party when I'd played the game, Seven Minutes In Heaven, and been forced into a closet with Stevie Steinway.

It had been the longest seven minutes of my life.

I wouldn't have minded seven minutes in a closet with Ian MacKinnon though, I thought with a shiver.

Ian's gaze shifted to something above my head. I followed his gaze to the charcoal drawing of Mount Hood, a mountain that had been visible from the living room of our house in Portland. I had drawn nearly all my life—practically from the time I could hold a pencil in my hand.

He came closer, still admiring the drawing, and I used the opportunity to stare at him, amazed at how every time I saw him he was even more beautiful than before.

"Such a lovely drawing, Riley. You're talented, lass."

"Thanks," I said, pleased by the compliment. "I drew it when I was fourteen. My mom entered it into a contest and I won first place." I can still remember how proud both my parents had been, displaying the drawing and the blue ribbon on the fridge for all to see.

"My mother enjoyed painting with watercolors," he said, pride in his voice. "She would spend hours at the easel."

"Do you, or—*did* you have any hobbies?"

"Of course. I enjoyed hunting, fishing, fencing and archery."

I smiled. "You sound like a man's man."

He laughed under his breath, his wide grin making my heart skip. "A man's man, hmm? I will have you know that I also enjoy poetry."

Now that surprised me. I would have never pegged him as a poet. "Really?"

"Yes, and I also enjoyed reading novels...when time allowed."

"When you weren't hunting, fishing, fencing, or shooting your bow." I couldn't keep the sarcasm from my voice.

"Exactly." A smile teased the corners of his mouth. "What about you? What other hobbies do you enjoy?"

"I used to dance. My mom enrolled me in my first class when I was five."

"And yet you don't dance any longer?"

"No. It was strange because I woke up one day and I was over it." My loss of interest in dance had only been part of the reason I quit, but mostly because I'd fallen in with Ashley and the wrong crowd. Our little group considered anything that didn't have to do with partying completely lame. Everything I had been passionate about had gone by the wayside.

"Life is too short to live with regret," he said softly.

I lived with regret every day of my life, and I doubted that would change anytime soon. "Do you have any regrets?" I asked, anxious to turn the tables on him.

He shook his head. "No."

I lifted a brow. "Oh, come on...everyone has regrets."

His shoulders lifted in a shrug. "Honestly, I had a good life, and all the hardships I endured only served to make me stronger."

I wish I could say the same, but I didn't feel stronger from the hardships I had endured. Instead, I felt broken.

"Can I ask you something personal?"

"Of course. You can ask me anything," he said, sitting down on the edge of my bed.

"Did it hurt to die?" I blurted, not wanting to dredge up bad feelings for him, but I was curious as to what my mom had gone through.

"Yes, there was pain, but it passed soon enough."

It wasn't the answer I wanted, and I instantly regretted having asked it. "I'm sorry."

He ran a hand through his silky hair, and I have to admit that I ached to touch the strands for myself—to feel the texture against my fingers. I wondered if he couldn't read my thoughts because he continued to stare at me, his gaze searching my face.

My mouth went dry. I recognized the heat in his stare. It was the same heat I felt rushing through my veins whenever I looked at him.

He suddenly glanced at the clock, as though there was someplace else he had to be. "Seriously, it is late and you need your rest."

"I'm not tired." I didn't want him to leave already. "Will you stay with me for a while?"

"I'll stay for a bit—at least until you fall asleep."

"You'll come tomorrow?" Oh my God, I was sounding borderline desperate, kind of like a needy girlfriend.

When I glanced at him, his gaze had shifted downward, making me aware that all I was wearing was a royal blue cami and boy-cut undies.

As I watched him watch me, I wondered what it would feel like to kiss him.

"Yes, I'll see you later today," he said softly, resting a hand on my leg.

I wished there wasn't a comforter and sheets between us.

"Goodnight," I said, trying to get my racing heart to slow down.

"Goodnight." Ian's voice was silky smooth, and his hand didn't move from my leg as he bent and kissed my forehead. "Now go to sleep, Riley."

Chapter Twelve

"Riley, you've got company!" my dad called from downstairs.

"Company?" I set the book aside, checked my reflection in the mirror, and wondered if I should change from my T-shirt and sweats into something nicer.

Deciding against changing, I headed down the stairs and was surprised to see Megan and another girl, who I hadn't met before, standing in the entryway.

"Ah, here she is," my dad said, looking elated that I had company. He had come home early for a change, but had gone straight to his study. Now he lingered, much to my annoyance.

"Hey, Megan," I said, giving my dad a look that said to please go away. "What's up?"

Megan's curly red hair was up off her shoulders, and she had on a lot of eye makeup. She wore a cute low-cut shirt, tight jeans, and five -inch heels. I wondered what the special occasion was, and hoped she wasn't going to ask me to go out. I wanted to wait and see if Ian finally showed.

I glanced at the other girl. Her long platinum-blonde hair was straight and had lots of layers. She had an oval face with a broad nose and nice, full lips. Taller than me, she was curvaceous, but not quite as busty as Megan. "Hey, I'm Cassandra," she said, her voice surprisingly husky.

"I'm Riley."

Cassandra nodded, and I felt a certain amount of hostility coming from her, which confused me.

"Cassandra and I thought we'd drop by to see how you were doing. I didn't get a chance to talk to you that much the other night." Her gaze shifted to my dad for a brief second. "I wanted to check and see if you had a good time."

She'd been so hammered, I had to wonder just how much of the night she remembered. I glanced at my dad, and lifted my brows, hoping he'd get the hint that he was embarrassing me in front of my new friends.

Apparently he got the hint, because he walked toward his study. "Well, it was nice meeting you, ladies," he said, keeping the door open.

"You too, Mr. Williams," Megan said.

"So, do you like Johan?" Cassandra asked abruptly, an obvious edge to her voice. Beside her, Megan stood up straighter and avoided eye contact with me.

Now I understood why they'd dropped by. It wasn't to befriend me, but to pump me for information.

I shrugged. "Johan's a nice guy and all, but I don't really know him."

"But do you *want* to know him?" Cassandra asked, crossing her arms over her chest and cocking her hip.

I crossed my arms over my chest. "I'm not looking for a boyfriend, if that's what you're asking."

Cassandra glanced at Megan and smiled. Megan's cheeks had flushed, and she looked ready to bolt. I remembered girls like her at my old high school, and I admit I was disappointed with Megan. I'd honestly thought she would become a good friend, but maybe I was wrong. I'd been wrong about so-called friends before...

"But why were you holdin' his hand then?" Cassandra asked, and it was all I could do not to walk to the front door, open it, and tell them to leave.

Instead, I lifted my chin. "I lost my balance, that's all. End of story."

"But he walked you home." Cassandra's voice sounded snarky and accusing.

"Yes, he did," I replied, ready to snap. "But like I said, *nothing* happened."

Megan turned to her friend. "See, I told you it was nothing."

Cassandra seemed to accept my explanation—but even then, I had the feeling she'd be keeping an eye on me.

"Why weren't you at the party?" I asked Cassandra.

"My parents only let me go out on weekends."

"A wise decision," my father said from his study.

"Excuse me a sec," I said, walking over to the study door. I shut it loudly, and both Cassandra and Megan laughed. Thankfully, it seemed to break up the tension.

Shane came down the stairs just then, and I noticed Megan straighten and fluff her hair.

"Hey, guys," he said, running a hand through his hair. "What are you up to?"

Cassandra immediately perked up. "We're headed to the glen."

"What's the glen?" Shane asked, checking her out. God, guys were so obvious.

"A place a couple miles up the road where we hang out and don't have to worry about anyone ruining our fun," Cassandra said, keeping her voice low.

"Do you want to come?" Megan asked, suddenly glancing at me.

Cassandra didn't look like she wanted me to come...but she did seem to want Shane there, because she grinned at him like an idiot.

Megan lifted a brow. "So, do you want to come with us, Riley?"

The glen ended up being a large meadow surrounded by giant oaks and towering fir trees. It was the perfect hiding place from adults, and now it was filled with about twenty-five teenagers.

In the center of the glen, a large fire blazed in a massive stone pit. A few of the guys had set their stereos on the roofs of their cars, the music blasting, but not loud enough that we couldn't hear each other talk. It reminded me of a place back home called Frenchman's Bar on the river, where we'd go every weekend to hang out with friends. We'd park our cars, sit on the riverbank, and there had been lots of drinking and partying. I remembered thinking life was so perfect. How little I knew that within months my world would be turned upside down.

"Johan's here," Megan said, nudging me and bringing me back to the present.

Johan stepped out of a sports car dressed in a black and gray pullover sweater and dark-washed jeans. He grinned and I had a feeling he knew exactly what that smile did to girls, myself included.

Ironically, I saw Ian's face flash in my mind at that moment. Although I had only just met him, what I was beginning to feel for him was more than friendship. I recalled the way he had looked at me last night—how his eyes looked darker, more intense, his gaze sliding down my body.

"Hey," Johan said, white teeth flashing, pulling me out of my thoughts.

"Hey," I replied, aware of others watching us. Apparently our spontaneous hand-holding at Milo's party had caused speculation. I felt stupid about reaching for his hand the other night, and wondered if I should say something to Johan about it. Or maybe it would be better to just make it very clear that I wasn't interested in a boyfriend.

"I was wondering if you were going to make it, Johan," Cassandra said from behind me.

Johan barely glanced in her direction, which made me curious what the story was with them. A one-sided attraction perhaps—or maybe they had been together. Whatever the case, the last thing I needed was drama.

"You guys want to play Truth or Dare?" a tall, slightly chunky guy with messed-up teeth asked. I recognized him from registration. He had stood behind me in line, and he'd been friendly enough, but I hated the way he'd stared at my boobs rather than make eye contact. Now he barely glanced at me, and even gave off a vibe that he didn't like me very much, which I found strange since we hadn't said two words to each other.

Twelve of us ended up playing Truth or Dare. We sat cross-legged in a circle close to the fire, including Shane who, holding on to a half-empty pint of whiskey, looked more than a little buzzed already. If I had to hazard a guess given his bloodshot eyes, I'd say he was blazed too, and I was worried how the night would unfold if he kept it up. After Milo's party, everyone probably thought I was a buzzkill and it was time to redeem myself if I was going to fit in.

The tall guy with bad teeth and attitude to match was Tom, and he had spent the past few minutes breaking up twigs, placing them in his fist, and holding them out to each player. Everyone in the circle drew a stick, and as luck would have it, I picked a shorter one. I breathed a sigh of relief when Shane pulled a long one.

Richie lifted the smallest stick and everyone laughed—a few people making cracks about it matching his dick size, which drew even more laughter.

"Truth or Dare, Richie?" Tom asked, crossing his arms over his chest and using his fingers to push out his biceps.

Richie narrowed his eyes. "Uh, let's go with truth."

"There was a break-in at the castle the other day. Were you responsible?"

My stomach clenched. I glanced at Shane. Our gazes met and held for a split second before he quickly looked away.

"No, it wasn't me."

A couple of people in the crowd teasingly called him a liar, but he lifted his hands, palms out, toothy smile in place. "God's truth, I wasn't responsible. I have an alibi. Ask your mum, Tom," he said in a husky voice. "She'll vouch for me."

Laughter erupted all around.

"Feck'n wanker," Tom said, shaking his head.

"Tom's dad is the police chief in town," Megan said under her breath.

I nodded, hoping his attitude toward me didn't have anything to do with his dad's suspicion or something like that.

"I didn't hear about any break-in," Megan said, and I sat up straighter, all ears.

"I heard my father talking to his partner about it on the phone." Tom cleared his throat. "Nothing was stolen, so that's why my dad figured it might be kids."

I hoped the case had been dropped. The last thing I needed was the police showing up at my door.

"Megan, you're next," Richie said. "Truth or Dare?"

"Truth."

"Word has it you kissed Cassandra at Russell's party last weekend. Is it true?"

I could see her face turn red in the firelight and knew the rumor was true. Megan glanced at Cassandra, who didn't look at all embarrassed. In fact, she flashed Johan a smug grin.

"Yes, I did," Megan admitted. "But I was really wasted."

The boys in the group hooted and hollered, and Milo high-fived the boy next to him. I never could understand why guys liked the idea of two girls kissing. I once saw a picture of two guys making out and it didn't excite me in the least.

"And I'm next," Tom said, puffing out his chest.

"Bring it on, Megan," he said with a cocky smile.

"Sure," she said, sitting up straighter. "Truth or Dare."

"Dare."

The crowd roared their approval.

Megan's eyes squinted as she looked into the darkness. "You must walk to the dueling tree...with your pants around your ankles."

A few snickered, but Tom stood up, unbuckled his pants, and dropped them to his ankles to reveal a pair of snug white boxer briefs. I was surprised he was so cocky given the size—or lack of— his package. A few of the other girls must have been thinking the same thing because they burst into giggles, and a few of the guys exchanged mocking grins.

Meanwhile, Tom started off toward the tree at a slow pace. The group watched, most laughing as he stumbled and fell on his face a few times.

I became nervous. It was my turn next and already my palms started to sweat.

Unfortunately it would be Tom doling out my punishment, and given his attitude toward me, I had a feeling he wasn't going to play nice.

By the time Tom made it back to the group, his face was flushed and sweaty. He pulled up his pants, zipped and buttoned them, before swiping his drink from his friend's hand and taking a large gulp, his throat convulsing with each swallow.

"Truth or Dare, Riley," he asked, wiping his lips with the back of his hand.

"Dare," I said, and the crowd responded with a few *oohs* and *ahs*. Clearly they had expected me to pick a truth question instead.

Assuming I'd be making out with Megan in the next minute or so, I fished for a breath strip in my jeans pocket.

Tom stared at me for a long, uncomfortable minute, which made me even more nervous. His gaze shifted to Cassandra for a second, and then he cleared his throat, drawing out my agony. "You're going to spend an hour in the mausoleum...alone."

The crowd went silent, except for a few people who looked excited and even a little shocked.

The mausoleum. Why had he chosen that particular dare for me? I wondered. And what had that look he'd shared with Cassandra been about? Had Megan told Cassandra about my interest in ghosts? I glanced at Megan and her sheepish expression said it all.

Damn, I had bad judgment when it came to new friends.

Megan opened her mouth as though to say something, but I looked away.

Apprehension rushed up my spine. "The mausoleum?" I said, just to confirm I'd heard him right.

"Did I stutter?" Tom said, one corner of his mouth lifted in a sneer.

What a dick.

"No fucking way," Shane said, shaking his head. "That's just wrong."

"Maybe you should go in her place then?" Tom dared.

"No problem," Shane replied, looking ready to rip Tom's head off. If he was a year or two older, I wouldn't have been so worried, but Tom was a lot bigger than Shane.

"It's my dare and I'll do it," I said, loud enough so everyone could hear me.

"That's not fair." Megan glanced at Milo, as though she expected him to help change Tom's mind. "He should pick something else— something less terrifying."

"Come on, Tom," Johan remarked. "She just moved here. We don't want to scare her off first thing."

I appreciated them coming to my aid and all, but I didn't want or need anyone's help.

"It's fine," I said, standing and steeling myself for what was to come. "I'll do it."

"Are you sure?" Tom asked.

I lifted a brow. "Did I stutter?"

"Bitch," Tom said under his breath, and it was all I could do not to knock him out.

"They'll lock the door, Riley." Megan pursed her lips. "There's no getting out once you get in."

"I get it, Megan," I said, not hiding my irritation.

She dropped her gaze again.

Tom waited with hands on hips. "What's wrong, not so interested in ghosts any longer?"

My heart sank to my toes. Megan had to have told them about the library books I'd checked out, because aside from me and Ian, only one person knew what books they were. I should have known. I was the outsider, after all. But I had to remember that no one knew I could see dead people, except for Miss Akin and Anne Marie, and I trusted them. But I couldn't trust anyone here. They were the kind of people who would put the new girl in a mausoleum alone at night.

Thank God Shane was here, because he was the only person I knew would have my back, and the only one I trusted...just as long as he didn't get wasted and forget about me.

Shane handed Richie his pint and stood. "This isn't cool, you guys. We lost our mom less than a—"

I shook my head, and Shane clamped his mouth shut...but it was too late. Everyone had heard him, and many looked guilty and concerned about the dare. Everyone except Tom, that is. He was clearly gloating, the heartless bastard.

"Riley, you don't have to do it," Megan said, taking my hand, but I pulled away. I was pissed off. She had pretended to be my friend, and had gone behind my back yet again.

I needed to be careful with her in the future.

Tom cleared his throat loudly, a mocking grin on his thin lips. I could tell he wanted me to bail, but I had to go through with it—if only to tell him to stick it, and plus, it was a good way for me to face my fears.

"I'll do it."

"This is seriously fucked up," Shane said, running a hand down his face.

"Someone needs anger management," I heard someone behind me say.

I wanted to defend Shane, but I already felt at a severe disadvantage. My fingers dug into my palms and I welcomed the pain.

"Ready?" Tom said, motioning for me to follow. The group all stood and started filing toward the cars. The cemetery was right up the road, and apparently everyone was going to make sure I went through with the dare.

"I'm going in with her," Shane said adamantly.

"No way." Tom planted his meaty hands on his hips. "She goes alone."

"Come on, Shane," I said, knowing he was ready to say something to Tom.

As I followed the others, I realized the enormity of what I had agreed to. I would be locked into the mausoleum in a cemetery where Laria was a resident. She hadn't necessarily harmed me, but would she have more power to do so in her territory?

"Hey, listen, none of us knew about your mum. You don't have to go," Johan said, coming up beside me. "Or I'll go in your place." He sounded sincere, and I appreciated the offer, but I would never do that to anyone. Plus, I needed to prove myself.

"Thanks, but I'm fine. I'm not afraid."

He watched me like he didn't believe me, and he shouldn't have, because I was scared to death.

"Has anyone ever spent time in the mausoleum?" Shane asked Megan, who appeared more concerned than anyone else. I think she was tweaked by Shane's outburst about our mother. She obviously hadn't expected that bit of information. Honestly, I didn't want anyone's sympathy, and I know Shane didn't either. In fact, he looked irritated with himself that he'd said anything about Mom. But he had, and to protect me, which really let me know we were on the mend.

"Ronald Green lasted about twenty minutes," Tom said with a satisfied grin. "He screamed his bloody head off until he was let out. Come to find out, he shit himself, and to this day he won't go near the cemetery. I don't know who or what was in that mausoleum with him, but whatever it was it really messed with his mind."

I could have gone without hearing that story.

"You're a fucking asshole," Shane said to Tom, who merely laughed.

Grabbing the pint from Richie's hand, I took a long swallow, much to the delight of everyone around me. If they only knew I didn't do it for show, but to warm my insides that had gone cold—and to give me the liquid courage to face whoever was waiting for me inside that mausoleum.

Chapter Thirteen

The graveyard was so dark I could barely see my hand in front of my face.

Tom handed me a flashlight, or what the locals called a torch, and wished me good luck, his expression saying the exact opposite. "No one is allowed past the gate," he said, pushing me toward the mausoleum, while the others stood back by the fence, their fingers curling around the wrought iron.

I glanced at my brother and he didn't look at all buzzed anymore, his eyes wide and alert, a nerve ticking in his jaw. "I'm not leaving, Ri."

"The rest of us will return to the glen so the police don't come poking around," Tom said, which brought mutters from the majority who obviously wanted to hang out and see what would happen. Did they expect me to freak out? If so, they'd be disappointed because I was determined to stick it out, regardless of who was in the mausoleum with me.

"That means at least two people need to stay to make sure she goes through with it...aside from her brother and Megan, because they'd probably let her out the second we left."

"Get stuffed, Tom," Megan said, not at all hiding her agitation with him.

"I'll stay," Johan said.

"Me too," Cassandra was quick to add.

Johan rolled his eyes and sent Cassandra an annoyed look.

"Only one car stays in order to avoid suspicion." Tom, who didn't wear a jacket, rubbed his arms and glanced at me. "Get on with it already."

What was this guy's problem?

Tom followed behind me, up the pathway to the mausoleum. It was the longest thirty feet of my life, and I tried my best to look calm and cool, which wasn't easy when on either side of the pathway gravestones loomed up to meet me. When at last I stood at the large, heavy-planked door, I experienced an overwhelming urge to turn and run.

Maybe it was my imagination, but I swear I felt the spirits stir in the cemetery and knew I wouldn't be alone tonight. I couldn't show fear, period. Not to Tom or the dead.

It would be a long hour, but I knew my brother wouldn't leave me, and if I yelled he'd be close enough to hear and help me out. Tom jimmied the lock off the door with an ease that surprised me. How ironic that a cop's son just happened to have the right tools to break in.

Tom pushed open the door and I flashed the light on the interior. Straight ahead of me was an altar covered by an emerald green velvet cloth. A huge candle sat in the center of the table in front of a gold, expensive-looking cross. A stained-glass window was high above the altar, and on either side tombs rose from the floor to the ceiling.

I swallowed hard.

"You can do it, Ri!" I heard Shane say just as Tom closed the door. It sounded like he slipped a chain lock on to the door, which made me believe he had planned this all along.

Seconds later I heard footsteps rush down the pathway, and then the gate opened and closed.

The cold air seeped right through the lining of my jacket, and I hugged my arms closer to my body for warmth.

An old, musty scent hung in the air, making it hard to inhale. With heart pumping like crazy, I walked toward the altar. I flicked on the lighter Megan had slipped into my pocket, and with trembling hand, I lit the candle.

The wick sputtered at first and went out. I tried again, and this time the flame caught and burned. I placed my hands above the flame to warm my fingers.

I could hear the footsteps of the others fading, car doors opening and closing, and then cars driving off, back to the glen. Although I knew my brother, Cassandra, Johan, and Megan were out in the parking lot, I still felt very much alone. "It's only for an hour," I said to myself. The space felt smaller by the second.

I took a deep breath, breathing through my nose and releasing it out of my mouth...just like my mom had taught me to do whenever I'd get a shot at the doctor's office.

My flashlight already started to dim, and I wondered if the spirits were using it for energy. I flashed the light on the bottom tombstones, and my heart lurched seeing the name MacKINNON engraved in the white and gray marble. The MacKinnon family were all buried here? I should have guessed given the close proximity to the castle. The dates started from the early fifteen hundreds. "Duncan, Kenneth, Grayson," I said, noting the dates on each. As I continued to the next line of graves, I realized how young these men were, most not reaching their fortieth birthdays, and in some cases, their mid-twenties.

I remembered my dad saying that life in the old West was tough, and if you lived to be thirty you were damned lucky. It must have been the same in Scotland.

Not finding Ian's name among the graves on that side, I turned and started searching the markers on the opposite side.

I was midway through when I saw IAN DAVID MACKIN-NON. My stomach coiled tight. "Born 1767, died 1786." The words stuck in my throat. "Beloved son, brother, friend."

I put my hand on the marble, my finger sliding along each of the letters carved into the stone. I'm not sure if I was feeling the sadness from the other family members, or if it was the fact I was so close to Ian's physical body, but tears welled in my eyes and tightened my throat. I wished he was here with me now.

Since arriving in Braemar, he had become my friend and confidant. He knew all about me, my ugliest secrets, and still he didn't judge me. "I swear I won't stop until I find a way to help you," I said, and from the corner of my eye, I swore I saw the altar shake. I held my breath, hoping it was my imagination, when the altar shifted again, causing the candle to fall over and the flame to extinguish.

My gut clenched as the silhouette of a woman appeared in the window—a window that was high above the ground. Either the person stood on a ladder...or they were just levitating there.

Don't freak out. Don't freak out. Don't freak out.

A deep growling came from what sounded like right behind me, an evil noise that had me too terrified to turn around.

To make matters worse, my flashlight died and I instantly flicked the lighter on. A huge gust of wind blew through the mausoleum and the flame went out. "Leave me alone, Laria. Go away. You're not welcome here."

The temperature dropped even more as I felt something slide over my head and tighten around my neck. A rope? I thought, grabbing at my throat. There was nothing physically there, and yet I felt an invisible noose that kept cinching tighter by the second. I found it difficult to swallow, let alone breathe.

Female laughter sounded all around me and I fought the fear that was beginning to consume me. Laria wanted me to panic. Instead, I focused on Ian and how I felt about him, on the comfort I experienced when he was near, and how together we would find a way to give him peace—a life free of Laria and her cruel curse.

The laughter vibrated the mausoleum, shaking me to the core. I closed my eyes and slid to the ground, hugging my knees to my chest. My heart pounded hard against my breastbone as the growling started again.

I positioned myself so my back was up against the wall, beside the altar, and below the window where Laria had been levitating.

I dug my fingernails into my legs and pulled upward, scratching the surface. I wished I had a razor with me. I wanted to cut—to focus on something, feel the blood form against my skin, and experience the release that always came after. I could feel the panic begin to take hold.

The pressure at my throat eased and the altar stopped moving. I looked up to see that the figure in the window had disappeared. An orb passed by me, up toward another grave. I reached for the flashlight and turned it on. It worked, but gave off little light.

MARGARET (MAGGIE) ETNE MACKINNON. 1744-1814. Ian's mother. I remembered the beautiful woman in the painting in the castle's dining room. Suddenly, a sense of peace washed over me, calming me. I found Ian's brother's and father's tombs as well. His sisters weren't here, which made me think they must have been married, and thereby buried along with their husbands.

I glanced at my watch. Only ten minutes had gone by, but it already felt like an hour. Remembering I had a new cell phone, I pulled it from my pocket, only to find I had no charge. Not a big surprise. Spirits used energy from any available source.

Knowing I had a long wait ahead of me, I grabbed the candle from the altar and took a seat beside the table closest to the side where Ian was buried. The fear that had gripped me upon entering the mausoleum and seeing Laria had lessened, and now I felt a strange calm. Setting the candle in front of me, I rested my hands over the flickering flame, savoring the little warmth it gave.

The orb appeared again, dancing in front of Maggie's grave.

"I see you," I said with a smile as it came closer. Suddenly, a cold rush washed over me, and I saw a flash, and then an image in my mind.

I remembered how Anne Marie had closed her eyes and focused on what the spirits were telling her. I did the same thing and at first struggled to see anything, but as I continued to focus and block out my surroundings, I saw a leather-bound book in my mind's eye. The vision quickly flashed to a dark room with a type of concrete floor that I didn't recognize, but I don't think it was the inn. The place in the vision felt older. The image flashed over and over again.

It was like I was watching a slide show. I saw a picture of the castle, and then Laria's face. She didn't look scary like she did now, but younger-looking, almost innocent. The vision shifted and I saw thick woods where a small crowd had assembled. Dressed in black cloaks that covered their heads, the group stood in a circle. Dread filled me as I heard chanting. A lamb was brought into the circle, and when a tall man stepped forward and pulled out a knife, I knew the lamb's fate. Without further ceremony, he sliced the lamb's neck, and filled a jewel-encrusted goblet with the blood. He drank from the goblet, then passed it to the next person, and one by one the gatherers drank.

A shiver raced along my spine.

Ian had said Laria had dabbled in the Black Arts and that's where the curse had come from. Was Maggie trying to warn me, or was she just showing me what I was up against—and how dangerous Laria was?

The image shifted again. Laria sat in a small room, writing in the journal, occasionally glancing toward the door. When she finished writing, she placed the journal beneath her cot, slid into bed, and blew out the candle on the small table.

The image faded and a mixture of fear and excitement rushed through me as I opened my eyes.

Chapter Fourteen

I heard a creak seconds before the door flung open and a dozen people were staring in at me.

"Has it been an hour already?" I asked, putting my hand up to ward off the glare of Shane's flashlight.

"Yeah," Shane said, relief shining in his eyes.

"Were you sleeping?" Milo asked. I could hear the admiration in his voice.

I hadn't been sleeping—more spacing off really, thinking about the visions I'd seen and how to move forward with helping Ian.

"She's got bollocks," someone else said.

Shane held out his hand to help me up. He was grinning from ear to ear, and when he hugged me tight I was surprised. Tonight he'd shown genuine concern for me and it felt incredible.

Cassandra seemed disappointed that I was in one piece, but not Johan. "Well done, you," he said, looking at me like a starving man stares at food.

I glanced over my shoulder and said a silent goodbye to Maggie and her family. I didn't look at Ian's grave. I couldn't without getting emotional. I just wanted to see him again and hug him.

I was still stunned at the visions I'd received and wondered if I'd had that ability all along. What if some of the bizarre, fragmented dreams I'd had in the past, which had never made sense, had actually been thoughts fed to me through spirits?

I'd always been so afraid of seeing the dead that I never considered that maybe they were trying to get my attention in order to help them.

Whatever the case, Maggie had given me clues to help Ian, and at least now I had a direction to move in.

As we exited the mausoleum, I felt an overwhelming urge to look at the castle.

My breath caught in my throat because I could swear I saw a body swinging from one of those trees. The head was twisted at an odd angle, and the woman's long brown hair was falling into her face, her arms limp at her sides.

I stopped in my tracks. "Oh my God."

I thought the words, but I must have said them aloud, too, because Johan looked at me strangely, then glanced over at the castle. "What's wrong?"

I shook my head. "Nothing. I just thought I saw something."

Cassandra snorted.

"It's probably just an animal," Johan said, squaring his shoulders.

I definitely wasn't going to tell him I'd seen a person hanging from the tree.

Shane grabbed me by the arm. "Come on, let's go home."

Right before we reached the iron gate that led to the car park, the gate swung wide open—and slammed shut a second later. Every person in the group let out a yell or jumped a foot. Everyone but me.

"Bloody hell!" Richie said, hand on chest. "What was that?"

An orb floated up and I looked around the group to see if anyone else noticed. They didn't seem to. They were too focused on the gate.

I smiled to myself knowing Maggie hadn't deserted me yet.

"Let's get out of here." Megan cowered behind Milo. "This is starting to really creep me out."

I forced myself not to look at the castle again. I didn't want to see Laria.

"Can you give me a ride home?" I asked Megan, who nodded.

"You're not heading back to the glen?" Johan seemed disappointed I was calling it a night.

"No, I'm done."

"I'll drop you off so Megan doesn't have to," Johan said.

"Megan already said she'd drop us off, but thanks anyway." Shane walked up to the gate that happened to open just as we got to it. He hesitated, but to his credit, he kept walking.

I was getting in the backseat of Megan's car when Johan grabbed my hand. "I was wondering if you wanted to go out sometime. Maybe see a movie one day this week?"

Just wanting to get out of there, I said, "I'll ask my dad and see what he says, okay?"

Cassandra walked past us, got into the passenger side of Megan's car, and slammed the door shut. She cranked the car stereo up loud.

Johan rolled his eyes. "Just so you know—we were never together."

I seriously doubted that given Cassandra's open hostility toward me.

Shane popped his head out the backseat window. "Come on, let's bounce."

I cleared my throat. "I, uh, better go. We'll talk later, okay?"

He nodded, still managing to look wounded.

I got in the car and shut the door behind me. Johan just stood there watching me until Megan got in and we pulled away from the cemetery.

Megan met my gaze in the rearview mirror and smiled.

Beside her Cassandra fumed. Her jaw was clenched tight. So tight she might snap teeth if she wasn't careful. Even though Johan denied any involvement with Cassandra, I wanted to ask her the story behind her relationship with Johan, but I hesitated because I didn't want her getting the wrong idea. Plus, we didn't have time because Megan pulled up in front of the inn a minute later.

Dad's study light was on, and when the headlights from Megan's car flashed in the room, I could see him moving inside.

"Shit," Shane said under his breath, grabbing a stick of gum from his pocket and popping it in his mouth. He handed me one.

"We'll see you later," Megan said, elbowing Cassandra who merely grunted.

Surprisingly, Dad didn't say too much as we walked through the front door, though he did glance at the grandfather clock in the parlor which read eleven on the nose. We were in an hour before curfew.

"Hey, you two, I'm glad you're home early. I wanted to let you know that I'm heading into Edinburgh tomorrow, most likely for the week."

"The week?" I said, not sure if that was good news or bad news with all that was going on.

"I can't get out of it, but Miss Akin said she was happy to stay here with you two."

The slight smirk on Shane's lips told me that he was thrilled by the news. He didn't make eye contact with Dad as he said goodnight and beelined it up the stairs.

I followed behind him when Dad asked, "Are you doing okay, Riley?"

If he only knew the truth…

I smiled to put him at ease. "Yeah."

"Are you making friends?"

"A few." *One being a ghost who has been dead for over two hundred years.*

He looked so relieved by the news, I almost laughed. "Goodnight, Dad. Have an awesome trip. Make sure you call and check in every once in a while, okay?"

"Thanks," he said, sounding happy I appeared concerned. "I'll check in every night."

I continued upstairs and held my breath in anticipation as I approached my bedroom door. I desperately wanted Ian to be there.

I opened the door and my heart plummeted to my toes.

The room was empty.

Chapter Fifteen

I had a tough time sleeping. Turning on my bedside lamp, I stared at the welts on my leg from where I'd scratched myself in the mausoleum. Since meeting Ian, I'd thought of little else but him, even cutting...which was a good thing. I just wish the craving to cut would go away completely. I hated the fact it seemed to linger in the back of my mind, especially when life wasn't going my way.

I reached into my nightstand and pulled out my iPod, put my earbuds on, and cranked the volume as high as it would go. The playlist was a compilation of all my favorite songs that I'd download-ed right after I'd learned we were moving to Scotland.

The music flowed through me, instantly putting me at ease. I wished I could scream the words at the top of my lungs. If it wasn't the dead of night, I'd head out the back door and run. Run until my legs felt ready to fall off. Run until the emotions welling up in me re-leased and I felt like I could breathe again.

My heart raced, and I glanced over at the dresser where I stashed my razor. I rubbed the tiny scar near the inside of my elbow, remembering how bad the pain had been when I'd cut on my arm before. It had hurt more than anywhere else on my body, which meant the release had been that much greater. It had also bled like crazy. Maybe I should make just a small cut...but not on my arm where everyone could see it. Maybe just on the inside of my calf again...small enough to take away the frustration I was feeling.

I slid off the bed and walked toward the dresser.

The song abruptly skipped to another and I glanced down at my iPod.

Oasis's "Wonderwall" blared through the speakers.

I stopped in my tracks. I didn't remember the song being on my playlist.

As the chorus repeated, a feeling of comfort and serenity came over me, and Ian appeared. He was so transparent I could see right through him, but I didn't care. He was here with me when I needed him.

I took my earbuds out and set the iPod aside. "I've missed you."

He smiled and the hair on my arms stood on end. "I've missed you, too."

"I think I know how to end the curse," I said, rushing on to tell him about the vision, terrified he would disappear before I finished.

"You believe the journal holds the secret to the curse?" His image flickered in and out.

"I do. Why else would your mom show me those things?"

At the mention of his mom, his brows furrowed.

"You don't speak with your family?" I asked.

"No, they've moved on. I have no contact with the other side."

Once again I was reminded of how lonely it must have been for him all these years—and how desperately I wanted to help him find peace. "Well, we just need a way into the castle."

"I can get you in whenever you'd like."

I nodded, ignoring the strange emotions rushing through me. If we found the journal and discovered a way to end the curse, then that meant Ian would move on and I would lose my friend, my confidant, and someone I trusted implicitly.

I would be alone again.

"We can take as long as you need, Riley. There's no urgency."

But there was. At least Laria was making me feel that way. I didn't know what else she had in store for me or my family, and I was terrified to find out.

"My dad will be gone all week, so maybe sometime in the next few days we can find a way into the castle."

"Yes, anytime. Just say the word."

I stared at him for a minute, taking in his features—the brilliant blue eyes, the long dark lashes, high cheekbones, and full lips. Kissable lips. My heart squeezed. As the days went by I was becoming more attached to him, not just as a friend, but someone I was attracted to—someone I wanted to be with. Someone who made me better than I was. Who helped make me whole.

I dropped my gaze.

"Stand up, Riley," he said, taking my hands in his own.

His hands were big, his fingers long, and I couldn't ignore the rush of exhilaration that flowed through my body at the contact.

"I want you to close your eyes," he said, his expression intense. "Close your eyes and keep your mind open."

I swallowed hard, closed my eyes, and did my best to clear my thoughts, but it was hard, especially with Ian so near, touching me, staring at me.

But soon I managed, and I was no longer in my room, but sitting at the dining room table at the castle. The room, lit by candles, had a soft glow about it, and there was laughter as everyone settled into their chairs.

Servants entered with steaming dishes, and I immediately recognized one servant. "Laria," I said under my breath, and Ian squeezed my hands.

It took me a minute to realize that I was seeing the room from Ian's point of view, and from Ian's time. I looked around the table and recognized his mother from the painting, and then his father, his brother, his sisters, their resemblance to Ian unquestionable.

Laughter filled the room, and I smiled at the warm sensations rushing through me. I was at home, safe, surrounded by the people I loved. I didn't feel like I had a problem in the world.

A tall, beautiful blonde entered the room, and I knew this had to be Murray's daughter, the family friend intended for Ian that Miss Akin had mentioned. My heart—or rather—*Ian's* heart skipped a beat, but I didn't get the sensation of him being head over heels in love. More like a crush.

I reached for the beer, brought it to my lips, and drank deeply. I wondered at the strange aftertaste as I set the goblet back down.

Almost immediately I felt woozy, dizzy, and a cold sweat broke out on my forehead. My heart raced against my breastbone and a strange pressure started in my throat and chest...a pressure that grew more intense by the second.

"Ian, what's wrong?" Maggie asked, her eyes wide as she looked at Ian's father with concern.

"Son, what is it?" his father asked, and the mood at the table abruptly changed.

Ian's brother stood, knocking over his chair as he reached for Ian's goblet and brought it to his nose. "Poison!" he roared, his gaze scanning the room.

Panic ensued, some of the servants rushing forward to help, others getting out of the way. Murray's daughter screamed and fled the room in horror.

A wave of dizziness washed over me, and I fell to the ground, convulsing uncontrollably.

Cries and screams filled my ears as Ian's mother cradled my head, rocking back and forth, looking down at me with desperation and helplessness.

"Catch the witch before she flees!" a man's voice said, the faces above me blurring as I coughed up blood, the metallic taste filling my mouth.

Maggie cried, her lips soft against my forehead. "I love you, my son. I love you," she said over and over again as cold seeped through me, deep to the bone, and I shook uncontrollably as the life left my body.

And then I stood back watching the scene take place, no longer an active participant. I realized I was now dead, watching helplessly as my family grieved for me. Sadness, panic, and regret washed through me, devastating feelings and emotions that everyone must go through at the moment of death...including my mom.

The image faded and I came back to myself and slowly opened my eyes. I hadn't realized that I'd been crying until Ian dropped my hand and wiped away the tears with his fingers.

I leaned into him, burying my face against his chest, my arms sliding around his waist, my fingers fisting the back of his shirt. I couldn't get close enough.

His arms encircled me, holding me tight. The experience had felt so real. All the emotions. All the sensations. Like it had happened to me.

"You are stronger than you know, Riley," he whispered. "You

have a gift, and don't you forget it."

He flickered in and out, and I felt his energy leaving me. "Please don't go," I whispered, desperate to keep him with me.

He kissed my forehead and whispered, "I must, but I'll return."

And then he was gone.

Chapter Sixteen

Miss Akin walked into the parlor where I was watching *The Notebook* with Megan, who had showed up at noon with a peace offering of cupcakes. I had a feeling she wanted to make amends for blabbing to everyone, especially Tom, about my interest in ghosts.

"Sorry to bother you two, but I was hoping you could help me out," Miss Akin said, flashlight in hand. "I keep losing power in the kitchen, and I need to check the fuse box."

"Where's the fuse box?" I asked.

"In the basement."

I thought all basements were eerie, but given the age of the inn, I could only imagine how creepy this basement would be.

"I can check the fuse box while you flip the stove on," she suggested.

Having seen how antiquated the stove was, I decided I didn't want to take the chance of touching the wrong thing and blowing us all sky high.

"We'll check the fuse box."

Megan's eyes widened. "Oh, no way."

"Come on, Megan. I don't want to go down there alone." I wanted to tell her if she could brave a cemetery in the dark, then a musty old basement would be no problem, but I wouldn't in front of Miss Akin. If Miss A knew what had happened at the mausoleum, she'd probably lock me in my room…or personally visit every parent of each kid that had been involved.

Just like my mom would have done.

The light to the basement was on, for all the good it did. It was a dark, cold, musty area with lots of places to hide behind, and I wondered if my dad had ever been down here. The steps weren't solid, and I envisioned someone standing behind those stairs, just ready to stick a hand out and trip me up.

"Gross," Megan said with a shudder, brushing at her arms. "Eew, there are cobwebs everywhere."

I laughed under my breath, clicking the flashlight on and off beneath my chin. "Wah-hah-hah."

Megan swatted me. "Stop it, Riley. Not all of us are brave like you, you know."

I'd never considered myself to be brave, but apparently an hour in the mausoleum had changed that.

"The old caretaker said the fuse box is by the water heater," Miss Akin said from the top of the stairs. "Give me a minute to get to the kitchen. When I'm there, I'll call out, and if you could, Megan, tell me when Riley has flipped the switch."

"Will do, Miss A!" I yelled, listening to her progress by way of the floorboards creaking overhead.

Megan hovered near the stairs. "I'm staying right here so Miss A can hear me."

"Rrrright…"

"Hurry up," Megan said, looking jumpy. "This place gives me the creeps."

"Doesn't everyone in town live in an old house?"

"Yeah, but not this old...and not this big." She gave a shudder. "I wish your brother was here."

I snickered. "I bet you do."

"What is that supposed to mean?" I instantly caught the defensive tone of her voice. Despite the fact she and Milo had been together for six months now, I could tell she liked Shane. She got all giggly and red-faced around him.

"Nothing," I said, walking toward the massive water heater. Sure enough the fuse box was nearby, and talk about antiquated. The box was large, white, and rusty, and let out a loud squeak when I opened it. I found the tag that read KITCHEN and reached for the right switch. "Ask Miss A if she's ready."

Megan yelled up the stairs to Miss Akin, who said she was ready.

I flipped the switch.

"Nothin'," came the reply a second later, from what sounded like the kitchen. "Flip the main switch, but be sure you have your torch on," Miss Akin called, her voice somewhat muffled. "We'll lose all the lights."

I flipped the switch and at the same time I felt hands slip around my neck.

"Very funny, Megan," I said as I reached up to pull her hands away.

"What did you say?" Megan asked, her voice coming from farther away, by the stairs...which meant it was someone else.

"The stove is on, girls!" Miss A yelled triumphantly from upstairs. "Well done!"

The ice-cold hands at my neck tightened, and I tried to pull away, but they held me firm, squeezing tighter by the second. Panic ensued. I dropped the flashlight and clawed at the hands around my neck. The more I struggled, the tighter the hands at my throat. I stepped backward, and felt a person behind me, and whoever they were, they were stronger than me.

"Riley, what's wrong?" I heard Megan, her voice full of fear.

I tried to respond, but I couldn't breathe and was getting dizzy.

"Forget him," an eerie voice said in my ear. "Forget him...or die."

"Riley, what's going on?" Megan said, her footsteps coming closer.

The hands abruptly released me and I gasped for breath. I had come close to passing out.

"Are you alright, Riley?" Megan asked, her voice anxious.

I held up a finger, signaling I needed a second.

"What happened?"

"I felt a shock," I said, feeling bad for lying, but I couldn't very well tell her I'd been attacked by a ghost.

"Oh my God, Riley. I'm so sorry. I thought for a minute there you were messing with me. You're lucky you didn't get electrocuted."

I nodded in agreement. "I'm fine now. I just need to catch my breath."

"Let's get out of here," Megan said, as she grabbed the flashlight, took me by the hand, and led me upstairs.

I scanned the basement as we ascended the stairs, and I didn't see anyone—until I glanced down and nearly screamed when I saw Laria standing beneath the stairs, watching us with a malevolent smile on her face that chilled me to the bone.

"Come on, Riley," Megan said, and I watched Laria as I continued up the steps. I refused to run...even though I wanted to.

Miss Akin met us at the top of the stairs, a huge smile on her lips that faded the second she saw me. "What's wrong? You're as white as paste...and what on earth is around your neck?"

Megan gasped. "Bloody hell, what's that?"

They were both staring at my neck.

I reached up, touched my throat. "What do you mean?"

Miss Akin pushed my hands out of the way. "You have red marks around your neck, like fingerprints." She looked from me to Megan. "What on earth happened down there?"

"Riley couldn't breathe for a second and said she felt a shock rush through her." Megan stared at my neck in the same way Miss Akin was.

I walked to the large mirror that hung over the fireplace in the parlor and lifted my chin. I could understand why they were so alarmed. Sure enough, there were purplish imprints from Laria's fingers around my neck.

"How can that be?" Megan said under her breath. "There was no one near you. It was just the two of us, and I swear to God, Riley, I didn't touch you. I was standing by the stairs the entire time."

"I know that, Megan. No one is saying you did."

Miss Akin gave her a reassuring squeeze. "My dear, all is well."

"It's okay, Megan," I said, but I could tell she wasn't buying it. She jumped when her cell rang.

Megan looked at the caller ID, flipped the phone open. "I'll be right there, Mum." She closed her cell and rushed toward the door. "I gotta babysit my brother. I'll call you later, alright?"

"Sure," I replied as the door closed behind her.

Miss Akin touched my neck again. "Who did this to you, Riley?"

I didn't know exactly how much to share with her, especially given how scared she'd been after the séance with Anne Marie. "I think it was Laria."

"Has she touched or harmed you before?"

"No."

She shook her head. "I should not have sent you downstairs. I should have just called a contractor."

"Laria could have done it anywhere, Miss A."

Miss Akin shook her head. "I do not like this at all. It makes me very uneasy. Even more so since I was supposed to meet with Anne Marie this morning for tea and she called to cancel. She hasn't cancelled in over twenty years. She's the healthiest, most active person I know—and now all she does is sit in her house all day."

"What's wrong with her?"

"I don't know. She said she had a cold. She sounded horrible—tired and worn out, but I sensed something else was bothering her."

I wondered if that something else had to do with a certain ghost who was making our lives unbearable.

Chapter Seventeen

There were at least twenty people surrounding me. All were dressed in black, monk-like robes, standing with hands folded together before them, their heads bowed.

I was pulled toward them by my captor, who shoved me into the hands of another cloaked figure. My captor rushed away, and the person before me pushed me to my knees.

As my eyes adjusted to the darkness, I looked around and recognized this place from Maggie's vision. The giant fir and oaks surrounded us, enclosing us deep in the woods, far away from prying eyes, which meant I was far away from any help.

My heartbeat was a roar in my ears, and grew even louder as the group began to chant, the words making absolutely no sense to me. Sweat poured off my forehead, and as the chanting grew louder, I struggled against the binds that held my hands together.

Terror gripped me, making it hard to even breathe. Was this it? Was I about to die at the hands of a cult?

A sacrifice...just like the lamb.

But now I was the lamb.

The person in front of me pulled out a knife, and the blade glimmered in the light from the fire. I felt the anticipation of the crowd around me, the way they came closer, the way their voices became louder, the chanting faster.

"Please let me go," I whispered. "I swear I won't say anything. No one will know."

The figure ignored me. He raised a hand to the others and the chanting abruptly stopped.

It was so quiet.

Too quiet.

There wasn't even a breeze. I was so tense, I jumped when the wood on the fire crackled and popped.

The cloaked figure lifted the knife high in the air.

This was it. I was history. I thought about my dad and my brother, and wondered how they could possibly handle such loss again.

The group resumed their chanting, in a strange language I didn't understand.

I concentrated on the voices, and I heard male and female voices—and even one or two that sounded young. Who would bring a kid here?

I swallowed past my painfully tight throat. "Who are you? What do you want from me?"

Silence met my question.

My stomach coiled as I was pulled to my feet and dragged over to a makeshift altar. Using all my strength, I jerked away from my captor and ran for the tree line, but with my hands tied behind my back, I was at a huge disadvantage. I could hear more than one person follow me. Seconds later, I was tackled and yanked over toward the altar.

I went completely limp, hoping to trip them up—but they dragged me back to the shrine.

One figure, slighter than the rest, came forward. He or she carried a goblet, similar to the one from Maggie's vision where lamb's blood had been drained into the goblet.

My fear was all-consuming, and I had to bite the inside of my lip to keep from screaming.

Within minutes I would be dead. I knew it with a bone-chilling certainty. These freaks would slit my neck, drink my blood, and life as I knew it would be over.

Finished. No more pain. No more loss. No more...

I fought against my captors again, which earned me a smack against the head. The side of my face throbbed, and I felt blood flow from a wound on my forehead.

I struggled against my bindings, and the ropes burned my wrists. I kicked the person before me and I was abruptly pushed back.

"Riley," he said sternly, and I stopped cold.

I gasped. Oh my God, I knew that voice.

"Ian?" I said in disbelief.

He pushed the hood back with both hands. His brilliant eyes were cold, cruel even, as he looked down at me with anger and hatred. "You must die now," he said matter-of-factly. Lifting the dagger, he fisted it with both hands and brought it down hard.

I came awake with a startled cry.

What the hell? The comforter was wrapped around my legs, and my T-shirt was soaked with sweat. I ran a trembling hand down my face. What was happening to me? Was Laria messing with me again? Were my dreams turning darker by the day because I was getting closer to Ian?

Shane whipped my bedroom door open. Baseball bat in hand, he looked around wildly. "What the fuck is going on?" He finally turned to look at me, obviously surprised to find me alone. "Are you okay?"

I nodded, too afraid to say anything for fear I'd burst into tears. The dream had seemed so real. As real as the vision of Ian's death, but this time it had been my death, and Ian, the person I trusted more than anyone, had killed me. I had felt all the emotions a person facing death must go through, and as much as the idea might have held some appeal, ironically, I wasn't at all ready to go. I had fought for myself, for my brother, for my dad. I'm not so sure I would have even a month ago, but I was a different person now. A stronger person, thanks to Ian.

Shane relaxed a little. "Are you sure you're okay?"

"Yeah, I just had a bad dream."

"You want to talk about it?"

I shook my head. "Not really, but thanks anyway."

He shut the door behind him, lowered his voice. "You shouldn't have gone into that mausoleum. Why didn't you just take a truth question?"

I didn't tell him why I was afraid of a truth question. I had too many skeletons in my closet, and I didn't want anyone here knowing anything about me. "Sometimes it's smart to play your cards close to your chest," I said, remembering Mom telling me that very thing shortly before her death. She'd been worried about me getting too friendly with Ashley.

He nodded. "Do you want me to crash out on your floor...at least until you fall asleep?"

I was surprised by the offer. Years ago, when he was about four, he'd come into my room whenever he was scared. Back then he'd just climb under the covers, a hand reaching out for me. I'd squeeze his hand, just smile to myself, roll over, and when I woke in the morning, he'd be gone, usually up and about, and neither of us said a word to our parents. "No, that's okay. The floor can't be that comfortable."

"I don't mind."

I could tell by his expression that he didn't mind. In fact, I think he needed to sleep on my floor as much as I needed him to. "Well, if you're sure you don't mind."

He actually smiled. "Just make sure you don't tell any of your friends."

"Trust me, I promise I won't say anything."

He went into his room and I took the opportunity to change out of my sweaty T-shirt. By the time I came out of the bathroom in a fresh oversized T-shirt, he was walking through the door with his comforter and two pillows.

"Thanks, Shane."

"No problem."

He curled up on the floor between my bed and the door, and we fell into an awkward silence.

"Riley?"

"Yeah."

"What happened to your legs?" he asked. "What are those marks?"

My stomach clenched tight as my mind raced about what to say. I didn't want to lie to him, and yet I couldn't bring myself to tell him the truth. I had lived in fear of the subject ever coming up. "When I was in the mausoleum I was a little freaked out and I accidentally scratched myself."

He swallowed hard. "Janie Anderson told me you cut yourself."

My heartbeat was a roar in my ears.

"I didn't believe her until one day when you left your backpack on the bus. Alex and a couple of his buddies went through it to see who it belonged to...and he found a blade. He swore to me that he would never breathe a word to anyone—well, except for Janie."

I remembered Alex, how sweet he'd been, especially after our mom had died. He'd been our next-door neighbor since his family moved across the street the year I'd started kindergarten. Janie was his equally sweet band-geek girlfriend.

"I *have* cut."

He flinched, and I could tell by his expression that he didn't want to believe it.

"But you don't anymore, *right*?"

I chewed the inside of my lip. "I don't want to anymore."

His brow furrowed as he thought about it for a few seconds. "I won't say a word to anybody, I swear."

"Thanks, Shane."

"If you ever need to talk about anything, just let me know. I don't want you hurting yourself, Ri."

Hearing the sincerity in his voice made my throat tighten. "Okay," I said, laying down as a myriad of emotions rushed through me, including embarrassment. It was one thing to own up to cutting to Ian who had caught me red-handed, but admitting I had a problem to my brother was tougher than I thought it would be.

"Riley, do you ever dream about Mom?"

My heart skipped a beat. "Yeah, do you?"

"Sometimes. Actually, I used to dream about her every night after she first died, but now the dreams don't come as often. In fact, half the time I don't dream at all."

"It's probably all that pot you're smoking."

He laughed under his breath, and I smiled at the sound. God, I missed that laugh. "Yeah, you're probably right."

He sat up, hooked his arms around his knees. "You don't have to answer me if you don't want to...but do you remember anything about the accident?"

The shrink used to ask me that question every single time I'd visit him, and I know my dad was curious about the details of that night, but he never pushed me. "No, I just remember waking up in the hospital and Dad sitting beside my bed."

Shane chewed on his thumbnail.

"I really am sorry, Shane."

He frowned. "About what?"

"About Mom."

"I didn't mean to make it sound like—"

"You didn't. I just feel responsible." My voice cracked and he was beside me a second later, hugging me.

"I should have just come home on time that—"

"Listen." His hands cupped my face. I had never seen him so serious before. "Mom's death wasn't your fault, Ri."

"But we wouldn't have been in the car at that minute."

"She could have been on the way to the store to pick up milk, or picking me up from practice." He hugged me again. "I can't imagine what it must have been like to have been there. It could have been me in that car. It could have been Dad."

But it hadn't been. It had been me, and I had to live with that guilt forever.

"Just know it's not your fault, Ri. It never has been. It never will be. I don't want you to ever think that I blame you."

My breath left me in a rush. I'd wanted to hear those words for so long.

"It's alright," he said, squeezing me tight.

I rested my head on his shoulder and let the tears fall.

Chapter Eighteen

Rohan drove his Peugeot with nice rims and tires through the winding Scottish roads like he was in a race. My blood pressure kept rising with the speed gauge.

I'm not sure if he was trying to impress me, but I was anything but impressed by the time we pulled into the parking lot of the movie theater in the heart of Aberdeen, a large city on the northeastern coast of Scotland.

In fact, I could have dropped to my knees and kissed the ground, I was so happy to be out of the car.

Milo farted, and Megan crawled out of the backseat, laughing and waving her hand in front of her face. "You're rotten, you know that."

Milo reached for her. "Ah, come on, my darlin'. It's not that bad. Show me some love."

Their playfulness seemed to ease some of the tension that had been building for the past hour. I was still mad that I'd been completely set up. A "movie with friends" had ended up being a double date. I was all about safety in numbers, but I would have been happier being a third wheel. This current situation is exactly what I'd been hoping to avoid.

Johan rounded the car, and I slid my hands into the pockets of my jacket. He fell into step beside me and put his hand on my back as we walked toward the theater. It wouldn't be so bad if I knew Johan just wanted to be friends, but I'd been in Braemar long enough to guess his reputation. I had a feeling he wanted more than friendship, and I was worried that I had given him the wrong impression the night of Milo's party when I had unwittingly reached for his hand.

I would just have to be brutally honest with him.

The movie ended up being just as uncomfortable as the car ride itself. Ninety-three endless minutes of Johan looking for any opportunity to touch me, and when he pulled a silver flask from his pocket and offered me a drink, I shook my head. He was ready to take a sip when I asked him what it was.

"Whiskey," he'd said, with lifted brows and a devilish smile, offering it to me again.

"But you're driving."

"Yeah, and..." he said with a dipshit smile on his face. "I'll just have a couple of swigs."

"The roads are windy and I don't think it's a good idea. Unless you want me to drive your car..." Not only was I not old enough to drive in Scotland, but they drove on the opposite side of the road.

He sighed heavily, screwed the cap back on, and put the flask back in his pocket.

Megan and Milo were oblivious, laughing under their breath throughout the movie, much to the aggravation of the couple in front of us. When they started making out, I couldn't help but think of Ian, and what it would feel like to kiss him the same way. Just thinking about him brought a smile to my face. Seeing him was the highlight of my day.

I jumped when Johan's hand slid to my thigh, and my stomach clenched with dread. This is exactly what I didn't want to happen. I opened my mouth to say something, but snapped it closed just as quickly. I could always push his hand away.

Megan leaned across Johan. "Riley, I have to use the bathroom. You want to come with me?" she asked, glancing at Johan's hand on my thigh.

Thank God.

"Sure," I said, jumping up and ignoring Milo's smart-ass remark about girls never being able to pee without reinforcements.

I used the bathroom, and when I came out, Megan was putting lipstick on.

She caught my reflection in the mirror. "So what do you think of Johan?"

"He's a nice guy."

"Nice as in you'd like to go out with him again?"

"Nice as in I like him as a friend." Oh my God, I was beginning to sound like a broken record. "Honestly, Megan, I wouldn't have come today had I known it was just the four of us."

"Milo's brother and one of his friends were going to come but bailed on us at the last minute, I swear."

I wanted to believe her, but given her track record so far, I wasn't so sure. "So since we're on the topic—what really happened between Johan and Cassandra? Were they ever together?"

Megan pressed her lips together. "Yes, and she liked him, but he's just not into her." She glanced at me. "It's probably just as well that you don't like him. He's a heartbreaker, that one."

Weren't they all?

"Can you keep a secret?" she asked, lowering her voice.

I nodded. "Of course."

"I mean it, Riley. You can't tell a soul."

I rested my hip against the sink. "I swear."

She lifted her pinky up to me, and I almost asked if she was kidding, but I could tell by her expression she wasn't.

We hooked pinkies and pinky-sweared, and I felt like I was in fifth grade all over again.

"A few months ago Cassandra and Johan started seeing each other. Just casually, but it grew serious pretty fast. He seemed to like her and she definitely liked him. He took her out, and well—she gave up her virginity, and then a few weeks later he drops her—just like that," she said, snapping her fingers.

"Back home we called those kinds of guys man-whores."

She laughed. "Johan *is* a man-whore. I mean, he can be a complete wanker, but he can be a nice guy too. The problem is he loses interest with a girl the minute he gets what he wants."

"Maybe one day he'll find a girl who breaks his heart and then he'll see how it feels."

"Yeah, that would be good for him." Megan dropped the lipstick in her purse. "I know Cass comes across as sort of a bitch but now maybe you understand why she acts like she does."

"I do."

"He really hurt her, and despite how she can be sometimes, she didn't deserve to be treated that way."

"Please tell her that this wasn't a date," I said, knowing the last thing I needed in my life was more drama.

"I will. And I'll be sure not to leave you and Johan alone."

"I really do need to get back early."

She laughed under her breath. "I'll just tell Johan I have to babysit my little brother."

"Thanks, Megan. I appreciate it."

"No problem. Hey, there's something I've been wanting to say. The night at the glen Shane mentioned that you lost your mum."

My stomach coiled. "Yeah, we did."

"I'm sorry, Riley. I'm sorry about opening my big mouth about the library books you checked out. It wasn't anybody's business, and I would have never said anything if I hadn't have been pissed out of my mind the night of Milo's party."

I nodded. "I appreciate the apology."

"If you ever want to talk about it, let me know. I lost my dad when I was four. I don't really remember him all that much, but I know what it's like to grow up with only one parent." Megan scratched the back of her neck. "And my mom is really embarrassing. She works at the village pub and borrows my clothes all the time. I swear she thinks she's still a teenager."

I was glad she was opening up to me, telling me things about her own life. "I'd like to meet your mom sometime."

"Hey you two, what the hell!" Milo said, popping his head into the bathroom, startling me, and making me wonder how long he'd been standing there. "The movie's been over for a bloody hour."

Megan rolled her eyes.

An old woman walked past Milo and shook her head.

"Sorry," Megan said, rushing toward him. "My mom called. I have to watch Liam this evening, so we have to get back."

"Ah, for feck's sake, man. She's always goin' out and leavin' you to watch the li'l shit," Milo said, not at all hiding his disgust.

"We can watch a DVD when we get back to my place," Megan said unapologetically. She kissed him on the cheek and he put his arm around her shoulders and pulled her close. "Just remember that I'm babysitting."

"Yeah right," Milo said with a smirk.

Johan walked out of the men's bathroom, a strange expression on his face, making me wonder if he'd overheard Megan and me talking.

On the drive home Johan kept sliding his hand on my thigh every time he shifted gears. Now that I knew the real story behind Johan and Cassandra, I was even more determined to let him know we wouldn't be anything more than friends. I just needed the right opportunity to tell him, and in a car with two other people wasn't the right time.

I breathed a sigh of relief as we approached Braemar. Within seconds we'd be passing by the castle and as we rounded the bend, I could see the familiar red stones peeking through the trees.

The painter's car was in the driveway, the front door wide open. Johan followed my gaze. "My cousins will be back in a couple of weeks, and I'll give you a tour, if you'd like."

My pulse skittered. "Your cousins?"

"Yeah, Kade and Cait MacKinnon are my cousins."

Johan was actually related to Ian? I didn't see that one coming. "That would be great. I—I'd love a tour," I said excitedly before I realized my enthusiasm might be misinterpreted.

Johan beamed as he looked at me, his eyes all soft and dark. Oh God, I knew that look. I quickly glanced away. His cousins would be back in a couple of weeks, which meant I needed to seriously get on with finding that journal.

As we passed by the cemetery, Laria appeared, right in front of the car. I put my hand up and held my breath. Johan swerved, nearly putting us through a fence before straightening the car out. He looked at me with wide eyes.

"Sorry," I blurted, embarrassed. "I thought I saw something run out in the road."

I looked in the side mirror and saw Laria still standing in the middle of the road, watching us, a satisfied smile on her face.

Damn it, I'd reacted exactly as she'd wanted me to.

"There wasn't a bloody thing in the road." Milo snickered in the backseat.

Megan elbowed him and told him to shut up.

"I'll take you home last, okay?" Johan said, his expression saying exactly what he had in mind.

I didn't get a chance to respond because he drove right past the inn and turned toward Megan's.

We dropped both Megan and Milo off at her house.

"Call me when you get home," Megan said before stepping out of the car.

"I will."

I swear Johan drove slower than the speed limit as he crept along the road toward the inn. "Did you have a nice time, Riley?"

"I did. Thanks for driving us." I was glad I'd paid my own way into the movie. That way no one could argue that this hadn't been an actual date.

"Maybe we can do it again soon."

"Maybe," I said, wishing I had it in me to tell him how I felt. I just knew how guys could be, and I didn't want Johan talking shit about me to his friends.

He pulled into the driveway and put the car in park.

"So...can I come in?" he asked, grabbing my hand and squeezing it tight.

I reached for the door handle and that's when I noticed someone watching us from the parlor window. My heart skipped when I saw dark hair and broad shoulders. Ian. I was so used to him coming at night that it surprised me to see him during the day.

Johan followed my gaze to the window. "Is your dad home?"

"No, he's working."

Excited to see Ian, I opened the door.

"Riley?" Johan sounded frustrated.

"Sorry, my dad won't allow me to have guys over when he's not here."

"I won't tell," he said, a cocky smile curving his lips.

"Miss Akin will, though. Seriously, my dad is completely anal when it comes to guys being here when he's gone. But I'm sure I'll see you around."

"Why are you being so hot and cold with me?" he asked, irritation in his voice. "Was Megan talking shit about me?"

Wow, he had gone from cocky and self-assured to suspicious and demanding in three seconds flat. "Megan didn't say anything," I said trying to pull my hand free.

His fingers tightened around mine. "There are two sides to every story."

Spoken like a guy who had something to hide.

I opened my mouth to tell him I really had to go when he leaned in and kissed me. His lips were hard against mine, and when his tongue slipped inside my mouth, I pulled away so fast I hit my head on the car window.

I stared at him in disbelief. What the hell?

"Sorry, I thought you..."

He thought what, exactly? That I wanted his tongue down my

throat?

"Too soon?"

Ya think? "Yeah," I said, pushing open the car door. He finally let go of my hand.

"Maybe we can go out again with Megan and Milo, so your dad doesn't think it's a date."

Ian was no longer at the window and I hoped he hadn't left because of the kiss.

"I gotta go. I'll talk to you later, okay?" Not waiting for his response, I rushed into the house. My heart slammed against my chest as I shut the front door and ran to the parlor, only to find Ian wasn't there.

I ran up the steps to my room to find it empty.

"Damn it," I said under my breath, mad that Ian had taken off before I'd had a chance to talk to him. I was so disappointed, I felt like crying.

"He likes you."

Ian stood in the doorway to the bathroom, leaning against the door frame, arms crossed over his chest. He was so beautiful, my heart skipped a beat.

I nodded. "I guess."

"He kissed you."

"I didn't want him to."

"Are you sure?" he said jokingly, but there was a slight edge to his voice.

"Did you *see* me pull away?"

"No, I wanted to give you your privacy."

I wanted to tell him that no one else could make me feel the way he did. That no one could ever compare to him. But didn't he know that? Couldn't he read my thoughts? Or perhaps he could only read certain thoughts?

The silence stretched out until I couldn't take it. "Oh, guess what—Johan is related to the MacKinnon family who live there now, and he's offered to give me a tour."

"Don't rely on Johan," he said abruptly.

I could read the jealousy on his face, in the way his jaw clenched. For some odd reason, the knowledge that he was jealous thrilled me. At least I knew my feelings weren't one-sided.

"He might just be our only way in...short of breaking in. I mean, maybe he can talk to his parents and get a key."

"We don't need Johan's help." I clearly heard the jealousy in his voice this time, and saw irritation in his eyes.

My stomach fluttered. "Then how do we get in?"

"I can get in anytime I'd like, but you, on the other hand, require a bit more finesse. Let me work on it."

I didn't think it could be too difficult for him to get me in, but maybe, like me, he wanted to wait awhile. Maybe—just maybe—he enjoyed my company as much as I enjoyed his.

He looked at my neck, reached out, and lightly pulled the shirt down. Only a tiny bruise remained. "Laria's going too far. This must stop."

"I'm not afraid of her, Ian."

He watched me closely, intently. "She is invading your dreams now?"

I didn't deny it. "I had a nightmare last night...and you were in it. Actually, you tried to kill me."

He frowned. "I would never hurt you, Riley. You know that, right?"

I nodded. "I know. I trust you."

Slowly a smile tugged at his lips, and the old Ian returned. "Have you read anything in the books about protecting yourself against evil spirits?"

I bent over my bed, reaching for the stack of books I had hidden there. All the blood rushed to my head, and when I sat upright, I realized my shirt had ridden up and Ian stared at the skin I'd unwittingly flashed him.

His gaze shifted slowly back to my face, and the blood in my veins turned hot at the heat in that stare.

I looked down at the book and quickly flipped through to the pages I recalled reading earlier. "It says here that small stones and pebbles placed along the floor can ward off evil spirits." I glanced up at him. "We can always go to the river. There are plenty of stones there."

We raced to the river and I picked up as many stones and pebbles as my jeans and sweatshirt pockets could hold. The sun was slowly slipping behind the horizon when we entered the inn again.

I unloaded the rocks the second I made it to my room, and Ian helped me place them around my bed and along the doorway and window frame. "I hope you know if Miss Akin walks in here, she'll think I'm crazy."

"No, she won't...she adores you," he said with a smile that curled my toes.

I stared at him, and I don't know what came over me, but I took the steps that separated us and I kissed him. I had meant for it only to be a chaste kiss, a *you-make-me-so-happy* kind of kiss, but it ended up being something altogether different.

I sensed his surprise, but only for an instant. The next thing I knew, his arms came around me, crushing me to him. I sighed into his mouth and he smiled against my lips before he deepened the kiss, his tongue sliding against mine, silky soft.

Exhilaration and need rushed through me as my hands flattened against his back. I could feel the play of muscle and sinew beneath my fingers. What I felt for Ian was real, and ironically he made me feel alive in a way I hadn't been since my mom's death.

Ian pulled away the slightest bit, looking down at me, his blue eyes intense. "We're playing with fire, Riley Williams."

"I don't care." And I didn't care. I wanted Ian MacKinnon more than I'd ever wanted anything in my life.

He opened his mouth to say something else, but I silenced him with another kiss. His long hair tickled my forearms, and as his hand moved down my back and settled on my hip, I moaned softly.

Footsteps sounded on the staircase and I held my breath. Ian put me at arm's length and started fading before my eyes.

"Don't you dare leave," I whispered at the same time a knock sounded at my bedroom door. It had to be Miss Akin checking in.

Her timing sucked.

"Tomorrow," Ian said, kissing me one last time, and before I could beg him to stay, he was gone.

Chapter Nineteen

I woke to the sound of scratching.

Exhausted, I kept my eyes closed, rolled over onto my back, and pulled the comforter tighter around my body. Unfortunately, it didn't keep the frigid cold air from creeping under the blankets.

I knew what that cold meant. I had a visitor, and I had a feeling I knew who it was.

With my heart pumping like crazy, I slowly opened my eyes and I wish I hadn't. Laria stared down at me, her dark eyes piercing, and her smile malicious.

My breath lodged in my throat.

"You wanted to know about witches and ghosts…and now you will." Her voice was low, eerie, a sound that terrified me as much as the circumstances I now found myself in. "Tell me, is it as wonderful as you imagined, or have you had enough?"

What the hell was she talking about?

Her head tilted in that odd, unnatural way that made my skin crawl. I knew she did it to freak me out and it was working, but I didn't let on. At least I hoped she couldn't see behind my false bravado...that was slipping by the second.

"But you do, and you should know better than to get involved in matters that are none of your business." She lifted her hand, flicked her fingers, and I was abruptly jerked from my bed and sliding across the floor. I couldn't stop—not by putting out my feet or hands. I was like a puppet on a string, and her laughter vibrated in my ears as I hit the wall with a bang.

It was a horrible sensation—like being in concrete and having no power over your own limbs.

Several more movements of her hands and I was sliding up the wall, my back stuck to the wall like I was a magnet on a refrigerator door.

Who knew a ghost could have such power, physical power—the power to do real harm.

My feet left the floor and I slid higher and higher. If I fell from this height, it would hurt. I might even snap a bone or two, including my neck. Maybe that was her intention all along—to kill me.

Laria watched me with an amused smile, and although I tried my best to hide my fear, it was impossible. I could hear my heart hammer in my ears, and no doubt she could too.

"Leave me alone, Laria."

"I can't hear you," she sang in an eerie, disembodied voice.

I tried to pull away from the wall, but it was no use. She lifted her hands and I slid further up the wall until I was on the ceiling, my hair hanging down around me.

Unable to look at her, I closed my eyes and thought one word.

Ian.

I bit my lip to keep from screaming as I slid across the ceiling. When I finally hit the opposite wall, I tweaked my hand hard. I didn't have time to think about the pain because I started sliding across the ceiling again, this time barely missing the light fixture. I could feel the heat of it though.

I considered yelling out, but Shane was spending the night with Richie, and Miss Akin slept in the guest room at the opposite end of the house with her fan on high. White noise put her to sleep and kept her asleep, she had commented more than once. She would never hear me. Plus, I didn't want to give Laria the satisfaction.

"Riley, open your eyes," she said, her voice coming from near-by—as though she was right next to me.

I didn't want to open my eyes to see if she was beside me, hanging upside down. That's one image I wouldn't be able to get out of my head.

I felt an icy hand on my shoulder, sliding up toward my neck. "Open your eyes," she whispered, her breath cold in my ear.

Ian, I need your help.

I began to move again, and this time I was thrust hard against the far wall, and then I began sliding downward, face first. My hair touched the floor, and I put my hands out in case she dropped me on my head, but a second later I was sliding back up the wall, toward the ceiling again. I felt the cool draft from the window and wondered for a horrifying moment if she'd thrust me out the window and hurling to my death.

I thought of the books I'd read about the paranormal, hoping to recall any of the books that might help me. Suddenly a phrase popped into my head. "You have no power over me," I said with conviction.

"Do you think words or stones can stop me?" she said, sarcasm lacing her voice. "You are a fool if you think so. You are facing someone with a power far greater than your own. You will never be able to control me. Forget Ian MacKinnon. Ignore him—and all will return to normal."

Forget Ian? I would rather die.

She must have read my thoughts because I was suddenly dragged along the ceiling once more, close to the light. I felt the heat near my thigh, burning the skin.

I clenched my teeth against the pain.

Then I heard a screech, and I was falling into strong arms.

I opened my eyes and looked into a familiar face.

Ian. He had come to my rescue.

He set me down on the bed. "Are you alright? Did she harm you?" he asked, looking me over, his gaze frantic.

I shook my head, unable to say anything. I'd never been so terrified in all my life. I'd just received proof that the dead *could* harm the living. I scanned the room. She was gone—and the heaviness had left with her.

His eyes were full of concern as his hands brushed over my legs and arms, checking for himself that I was okay.

"She won't hurt you any more, Riley. I won't allow it."

I forced a smile and rested my head against his shoulder. He lay down beside me, holding me close, and I wondered how long he would stay this time. I hated that our time together was always so short.

"Try to sleep," he whispered, his fingers grazing my jaw.

"You always say that when you come to my room," I said, turning off the light and settling into his arms.

When I awoke, the clock radio read four twenty-three. Ian still held me and I turned in his arms, happy he was still with me. His eyes were open and he smiled softly as I burrowed closer.

I reached under his shirt, feeling the hard muscles of his back beneath my hand. I knew I was being aggressive, but I didn't care. I also knew the danger to my heart in taking our relationship further, and yet I kept wondering what would happen if I died tomorrow, which was a very real possibility given Laria's vendetta against me now that I was helping Ian.

The truth was that I ached to explore his body. I wanted to be with him, Ian, this *ghost* I trusted more than anyone else. I kissed his neck, his ear, his jaw. My hand wandered to his wide chest, and down over the sculpted muscles of his abdomen.

His hand rested on my hip, his long fingers drawing upward along my side. He cupped my breast through the material of my shirt and bra, and my breath caught in my throat.

I felt his hesitation only for an instant, before he rolled and covered my body with his, taking his weight on his elbows as he stared down at me. Every inch of his body was pressed against mine.

His long, silky hair tickled my collar bones. He had never looked so beautiful to me as he did in that moment, his eyes heavy-lidded in a way that had me aching to discover everything that could happen between a man and a woman.

I touched his strong jaw, my thumb brushing along his lower lip. He pressed his face into my hand, placing a kiss against my palm.

"Riley, what are we doing?" he asked, his voice silky soft.

"Isn't it obvious?"

He closed his eyes for a few seconds, took a deep breath, and rolled off me, onto his back, resting his hands against his forehead. "We cannot do this, Riley. It's dangerous."

I went up on an elbow. "I don't care if this is all we have. I'd regret it more if we didn't do anything."

He glanced at me, and I could see the desire in his eyes. My pulse skittered with the realization that he wanted me as badly as I wanted him.

"I want to be with you, Ian," I blurted before I could stop myself.

He swallowed hard. "I want you too, Riley."

His words eased my fears, but I could still see the indecision he was feeling in his expression.

"Then what are you so afraid of?" I asked, terrified of the answer.

He reached up, cupped my face with his large hands, and said, "I'm afraid of not being able to leave you when the time comes."

Chapter Twenty

When I reached the top of the hill, I turned and took in the view. It was even more incredible in person than it had been in the dream...green as far as the eye could see, hills full of heather, and a gently rolling river that cut a path right through the town.

I looked toward the castle with its turrets and spires and tried hard not to remember every detail of Ian's death. I instead thought about what it must have been like to grow up in such a place. A life without the Internet, cell phones, television, and game systems. A life so different from my own.

I thought again about last night, about the look in Ian's eyes when we'd kissed, the surprise and the desire I had seen there—the same desire that had rushed through my veins. He had touched me, something I'd never let any other guy do, and it had felt amazing. Amazing in a way that made me giddy and excited to see him again.

Smiling at the memory, I took off the backpack and spread out the sweater that I had tied around my hips. I sat down and pulled out the book Miss Akin had left on my dresser while I was taking a shower, and flipped through the pages. My heart leapt when I saw the MacKinnon name. It took me all of ten seconds to find Ian's family. I touched each name, feeling a kinship with this family I had only met through a vision. I had felt their love for Ian though—as well as their intense sadness and their anger toward the woman who had taken him away.

I skimmed the passages about the family and smiled as I read about Ian's father and the love affair with his mother.

My pulse skittered when I read:

The eldest son, Ian David MacKinnon, had many talents—he was an accomplished marksman, swordsman, and had a great love for art and poetry.

I grinned, remembering him telling me the same thing—well, except for the art. Little wonder he had noticed my drawing.

Sadly, he was murdered at the age of nineteen. A servant, a jealous lover it is said, had poisoned him. The MacKinnon family never spoke of the servant, saying that one day she left and never returned. Rumor says the family sought their own retribution, and her body was buried just beyond the cemetery, on unholy ground, but to this day those rumors have never been proven.

A shiver rushed through me and I glanced up, looking past the cemetery, wondering exactly where Laria's body had been buried.

I shut the book, not wanting to read any more. I remembered the vision Maggie had pushed at me, and despite the fact I wanted to keep Ian with me, I knew I needed to work at ending the curse. I couldn't keep him here for my own selfish reasons.

I glanced at the castle. Ian could get in anytime, but how did I get in without being noticed? Since the castle sat just off the main highway, it would be tough to get in during the day. I didn't see any cars there now, and the only person I had noticed coming or going had been the contractor. But that didn't mean someone wasn't watching, especially after the last break-in.

I needed to set a plan in motion and read everything I could on protecting myself from witches and evil ghosts. The stones hadn't exactly helped. In fact, it seemed to only make Laria angrier. Maybe I would visit Anne Marie and see if she had any suggestions.

My gaze shifted back to the village. I had done okay since coming here. I would be okay. I felt it in my bones, even as I ignored the sharp ache in the pit of my stomach knowing soon I would be alone again, and Ian would be where he belonged. It would hurt like hell to let him go.

He had shown me that maybe, just maybe, I could use my gifts in a way that could help people.

Leaning back on my elbows, I closed my eyes and lifted my face to the sun. The warmth felt wonderful—and I sighed, focusing on Ian. I wanted to connect with him, wanted to spend every second, of every minute, of every day with him until he passed over.

A shadow fell across me and I opened my eyes.

My heart swelled. It was Ian, staring down at me, his arms crossed over his wide chest, his long hair fluttering in the breeze.

"Doing a bit of reading, I see," he said, with a devastating smile that made my insides tighten.

"Yeah, a bit."

I couldn't help but remember last night, the kiss we had shared, how hot the moment had been—and how I wanted to do so much more.

He sat down beside me and rested his arms on his knees. "A beautiful view, is it not?"

I nodded. "It's breathtaking," I said, remembering I'd said the very same words in my dream.

"I can spend hours up here."

My pulse skittered. This conversation was all too familiar. I didn't want a repeat of that dream, of him jumping off the cliff. "Did you come up here a lot?"

"All the time."

"I can see why."

I could tell by his expression that he liked my response.

The breeze whipped his hair, and I couldn't resist—I reached up, touched a strand, and wrapped it around my finger. He turned to me, his eyes searching my face, like he was memorizing my features.

Before I could blink he leaned in and kissed me.

His tongue was like satin against mine, his lips gentle, yet firm. One of my hands rested on his chest, and ever so slowly drifted down, toward his chiseled abdomen. A hot ache grew inside me, more intense by the minute.

I was so confused by the warring emotions running through me. I wanted him with a desperation that frightened me, and yet I wanted to help him, to let him pass on and know peace.

But his peace would require me letting him go, and I didn't know if I could do that right now. What would it hurt for us to continue as we were now? Sure, we could never be boyfriend and girlfriend in the traditional sense—walking down the school halls hand in hand, or hanging out with friends—but his companionship was as real to me as any relationship I had.

He pulled away abruptly and looked toward the castle, then to the cemetery, and finally to the inn.

The hair on the back of my neck stood on end, and I knew Laria had found us.

He put up a finger, listening intently. "Do you hear something?"

I shook my head. "What do you hear?" I whispered.

"Singing."

"Maybe Miss Akin is outside hanging laundry. She norm—"

"It's not Miss Akin," he interjected. "Focus, Riley. Close your eyes and tell me what you hear. Tell me what you feel."

I did exactly as he asked, closing my eyes and listening. Immediately a heaviness came over me, a cold blast that shot through me. Then ever so faintly, I heard singing. I opened my eyes and Ian was watching me. "It's Laria," I said and he nodded. I wished she would give me peace, but I knew the closer Ian and I became, the more Laria would fight me.

Ian stood, reached for my hand, and helped me up. "It's not safe to be here now."

His expression made me nervous, and I didn't waste any time pulling my things together. I threw the book and my sweatshirt into the backpack, and slung it over my arm.

He took my hand, and I fell into step beside him. I had to speed walk just to keep up with his long strides.

The singing stopped abruptly but Laria's interference had been felt, and had completely ruined the moment we'd shared on the hill. I wondered what she would do if we ignored her. Would she eventually just go away, much like the old lady ghost had done when I had ignored her?

Someone pushed me from behind, so hard, I would have fallen flat on my face if Ian hadn't have been holding on to my hand. Laria's cruel laughter followed me.

"Leave her alone, Laria," Ian said, his voice angry, his jaw clenched tight. "She hasn't done anything to you. Your fight is with me."

Unfortunately, I had inadvertently joined their eternal fight, and

I needed input on how to move forward.

I squeezed his hand. "I have a friend who might be able to help us."

Anne Marie lived in a small brick house on acreage just outside of Braemar, with four cats and a wiener dog named Diggs that followed me around and barked at Ian, who stood just outside the front door.

Ian said he didn't want to come inside because he was afraid of distracting me, and I was glad he didn't come in...because he *did* distract me. My thoughts were in turmoil where he was concerned, and no matter what I did from this point on, the end result would be the same. He was not my boyfriend, and he never would be.

"I'm so glad you dropped by, my dear. I was most concerned about you."

"I was concerned about you, too," I said, closing the front door behind me. "Miss Akin said you weren't feeling very well after your visit."

"Ah, she worries too much."

We entered her small living room that was cluttered with an organ, a well-worn couch, a rocker, and a tall wooden rack with a crazy collection of salt and pepper shakers. "Would you like a cup of tea, my dear?"

"No, that's okay." Since the entire country drank tea, I wasn't about to tell her I didn't like the taste of it. Maybe in time it would grow on me.

"Have a seat, my dear, and I'll be right in. You sure I can't get you anything?"

"I'm fine. Thanks, though."

She disappeared into the kitchen. I sat down on the couch and Diggs immediately jumped up on my lap. He looked toward the porch, in the direction of Ian, who sat on the porch railing. His arms were braced on either side of him, and his long legs stretched out in front of him and crossed at the ankle. He looked like he could be modeling for a Ralph Lauren ad. My heart swelled with love and desire for him.

Diggs barked, and Ian looked our way and smiled.

I felt that grin all the way to my toes.

"I have a feeling you have something on your mind," Anne Marie said, sitting down in the rocking chair. She took a sip of tea and set the cup down with a shaky hand. "Are things getting worse for you?"

I was terrified of telling her too much in fear Miss Akin wouldn't let me out of the house. On the other hand, she was the only other person I knew that had similar abilities as me, and I desperately needed input. "I suppose you could say things are getting worse."

She nodded. "Is it Laria?"

My pulse skittered. "Yes."

"I can't say I'm surprised, given the fact she's been visiting me on a regular basis since our séance."

I didn't want to hear that. It was bad enough that Laria was making my life difficult. I hated to think I'd brought this upon someone else who was just trying to help me. "What does she do when she visits?"

"She mostly invades my dreams, and when I wake I feel her presence with me. I have asked if she needs help passing over."

"And has she ever said anything?"

"No, but I feel her—and Diggs sees her, too. He doesn't like her and he is an excellent judge of character," she said matter-of-factly.

"Good dog," I said, patting his belly, much to Anne Marie's amusement.

"I'm sorry, Anne Marie. I wish I would have never said anything about Ian or his family to Miss Akin. I should have just kept this to myself."

Her eyes narrowed. "Nonsense," she said, shifting in her chair. "You should not have to bear the brunt of this alone when there are those who can assist you. Miss Akin adores you and she will do everything in her power to help you, just as I will."

Which reminded me why I came to Anne Marie's in the first place. "Actually that's why I'm here. Do you know a way I can protect myself against Laria and other evil spirits?"

"Yes, I have tried several herbs of late, ranging from garlic to willow, but I don't think herbs alone will be strong enough to deal with this spirit. Do you own a cross necklace?"

"Yes, I have one in my jewelry box."

"I suggest you wear it night and day. And I would visit the old medieval church in town. The priest keeps blessed holy water in a marble bowl near the altar. I would fill a small bottle or vial with it and keep it with you at all times. This should ward off any evil spirits and protect you from harm."

Already I felt better, stronger, and as much as I wanted someone like Anne Marie to help me, I needed to do this alone. I didn't want to be responsible if Laria hurt anyone.

By the time I left Anne Marie's house, the sun was starting to set. Ian and I walked to the old church, and I filled the small vial Anne Marie had given to me before I left with holy water. I slid it in my pocket, hoping it would help keep Laria away.

Chapter Twenty-One

It was so dark outside—I could barely see my hand in front of my face. A good thing I had Ian with me to lead the way.

I had dressed for the occasion wearing all black from head to toe, and even borrowed one of Shane's stocking caps to cover my hair.

"You're trembling," Ian said, taking my hand within his own as we walked onto the castle grounds. His presence comforted me and gave me strength. He was the reason I was here, I kept reminding myself, trying not to think of life without him.

The castle had never looked more ominous, plunged in darkness, the trees surrounding us whipping in the breeze. It was also freezing, and the wind cut right through me. I couldn't get close enough to Ian if I tried.

I wondered what was awaiting us tonight. Would we find the journal and be that much closer to finding answers, or was Laria already waiting for us?

At least I'd taken Anne Marie's advice and worn the cross necklace, and I had the glass vial of holy water in my pocket.

I don't know what more I could do to protect us.

Ian squeezed my hand. "I'll not let anything happen to you, Riley."

I trusted him completely. The problem was, I didn't trust Laria. I hated that she had been haunting Anne Marie, and I wondered about her motivation. What would she have to gain by scaring an old woman who had little to do with me, save for having similar abilities and being friends with our housekeeper?

"I'll be just a second," Ian said, walking straight through the castle wall and opening the window. I slipped in and he led me straight toward the servants' quarters.

I hated sneaking into the castle again. If I were caught, a breaking-and-entering charge would be the least of my problems. I had no idea if I could explain to my dad, or the cops for that matter, why I had done it. If I said anything about searching for an eighteenth-century journal that belonged to a witch who had cursed the ghost I had fallen in love with, my dad would have me committed on the spot.

I held on tight to Ian's hand, but it didn't stop me from tripping over my own feet while trying to manage the spiral steps in the dark. I had a flashlight in my back pocket, but I was afraid to turn it on in case a passerby saw it. I didn't want to alert anyone to my presence, especially since the recent break-in.

A part of me wanted to tell Ian to search the basement while I checked out the upstairs, but I was scared of splitting up. Terrified to turn around and find Laria staring back at me.

She had gotten under my skin in a big way, and I didn't know how far she would go in stopping me. Despite the precautions I'd taken with the herbs, the cross necklace, and the holy water, I was still intimidated by her after the whole ceiling episode and I always wondered what she would do for an encore.

"The attic is full," Ian said, shoving the door open.

He wasn't kidding. My stomach knotted seeing boxes stacked on top of boxes. It would take days to go through everything here, and overlooking something as small as a journal would be easy. Thankfully, there was a window that allowed some moonlight in, and I flipped the flashlight on.

Ian was searching along the floorboards, which reminded me of what I had seen in the vision. The floor hadn't been wood.

"I don't think this is it," I whispered. "It was a solid floor, kind of like concrete or maybe stone."

"Then let's check the basement," he said, taking me by the hand and leading me back down the stairs.

We were just a few steps away from the landing when I heard a loud knocking noise. We stopped in our tracks. Ian put a finger to his lips and I nodded, my heart thudding hard against my chest.

I prayed it wasn't someone at the front door. Oh God, what if it was the police? What if someone had seen me break in?

The knock sounded again, this time from above us, suspiciously close to the room we had just been in.

From the corner of my eye I saw the sword on the wall shift. I gasped and moved out of the way, pulling Ian with me. A second later I heard a *whoosh* as the sword fell to the ground, missing me by inches.

Ian urged me forward, and I nearly tripped over my feet in my rush to get away.

The knocking started to intensify, growing louder, more consistent, and all over the place...just like at my house during the séance with Miss Akin and Anne Marie. I wanted to cover my ears, but I forced myself to ignore it as best I could, and focus on the task at hand. We had one shot at this given the family was returning soon.

"Don't worry, we'll find it," Ian said softly as we entered the basement.

I walked down the same hallway from my previous visit and looked into each room, hoping something looked familiar from the vision. I did my best to focus and keep my mind open.

Glancing into a room full of odds and ends of furniture and workout equipment, I noticed an old-fashioned chest that sat beneath a window, and it instantly triggered my memory.

"The chest." I flipped on the flashlight, looked at Ian. "I think this is it."

The sensation that I was on the right track felt stronger the closer I came to the chest. I went down on my knees beside it. There was no lock on the clasp. My hands trembled as I lifted the lid. Instantly my heart plummeted. The chest was bulging with various items, many wrapped in tissue paper.

I immediately started unloading the items and Ian helped me, carefully setting each aside. "Hey, I meant to ask you something that's bothered me about the journal and Laria. I was under the impression that servants back in your day didn't read, especially women."

He nodded. "You're right—many servants didn't know how to read or write, but my mother felt education was important, and so she had a teacher come in once a week so that the servants could learn to read and write."

"Your mom sounds like a kind-hearted soul."

He grinned. "Yes, she was."

I had the chest nearly emptied out when I saw an object that was roughly the same size as the journal I had seen in the vision. "I think this is it," I said to Ian, whose eyes widened.

With trembling hands, I picked it up and unwrapped it. My heart raced as I stared down at the brown leather journal that I had seen in my vision. Excitement rippled along my spine.

A high-pitched scream pierced the quiet, making me nearly jump out of my skin.

I grinned at Ian. We had done it.

Ian lay beside me on my bed and was fading faster by the second. He had used up so much energy at the castle, and now I brushed my fingers through his soft hair, frustrated that he would be leaving soon. I wanted him to stay with me forever. I was terrified of going back to the way life had been before he'd come rushing into it. Lonely, sad, depressing.

The journal was on my nightstand. I had flipped through it earlier, but finally put it aside when Ian had grown quiet. He'd seemed almost...disinterested. What was he feeling, I wondered? Was he scared about moving on? Did he worry about what awaited him on the other side?

I wound a strand of his hair around my finger. The corners of his mouth curved slightly as he stared at me, but his eyes looked sad. Even more unsettling, the way he watched me made me think that he was trying to memorize my features.

"What's wrong?" I asked.

He shook his head, took my free hand, and brought it to his lips where he softly kissed the backs of my fingers.

My mouth went dry.

I sensed there was something he wanted to say. There was so much *I* wanted to say, but I couldn't bring myself to say the words.

"Will you come tomorrow?" I asked.

He flickered in and out. "Yes," he said, and faded before my eyes.

I fell back onto the bed and sighed at the ceiling. God help me, but I had fallen head over heels in love with a ghost. Ian was as real to me as anyone, but to everyone else he was dead. Fighting back tears, I ran my hands down my face.

I picked up the leather journal and fought the need to hurl it against the wall. Cussing under my breath, I turned to the first yellowed page. It smelled musty and old. Holding the journal in my hands, I couldn't help but envision the author of the words, sitting in her small room, scribbling away.

Laria. It was difficult to remember that the creepy ghost who had been haunting and scaring the hell out of me had at one time been young and innocent. A girl who had fallen for a boy who could never be hers. I still wondered at the extent of her relationship with Ian, but there was a part of me that didn't want to know everything.

April 11, 1786

Today I am no longer a scullery maid, spending my days on hands and knees, and working until my hands crack and bleed. Now I am the cook's assistant, and already I believe she is pleased. Tomorrow I shall work extra hard in the hope that one day I will attain the position of lady's maid. Father told me he is very proud.

April 18, 1786

I am so very weary. Never did I realize working as a cook's assistant would be so tedious. I wake before dawn, and spend the first hour of my morning gathering eggs and hauling milk to the kitchen. The buckets are so heavy, but I try not to complain. Cook does not let me help with any of the actual cooking yet, but I feel in time if I prove myself worthy, that she will. The MacKinnons' sons return from their travels tomorrow, which means all servants have been asked to lend a hand with the preparations. It is quite the celebration since they have been away for years now. I have requested to help serve at dinner. I believe Cook is considering this, since she has asked if I have a nice dress to wear. I hope I am chosen!

April 19, 1786

I served the family tonight. I was so nervous I nearly spilled the soup all over the eldest son. I remember him as a handsome boy, but never did I dream he would grow to be such a beautiful man. Eyes of blue and hair darker than midnight, he had all the female servants aflutter. Such a charming man! His younger brother is handsome as well, but much more quiet and reserved.

May 1, 1786

I LOVE IAN MACKINNON.

My insides twisted at the bold words staring back at me. I took a deep breath and continued reading.

I can think of little else but him. Indeed, it is difficult to get through my duties each day. I yearn to be with him and must be careful to keep my thoughts to myself, for my father would never approve. He would say I have reached too high for my station, but I do not care. I want only to be with Ian.

I quickly flipped the page.

May 3, 1786

Tonight I meet with the others. Father would be horrified to know I am involved with such individuals, and yet I am intrigued by what I have learned so far. In fact, I believe the elixir has made a difference with Lady MacKinnon's cough. Indeed, I hope by helping her she will look at me more favorably, and perhaps one day I shall serve as lady's maid to her or one of her daughters.

May 11, 1786

The past week has been wonderful. I have spent an hour of each night with Ian. He reads poetry to me, and I have found him to be a thoughtful and compassionate companion.

May 21, 1786

I have not written in some time. My duties have kept me busy, and life was wonderful until Margot Murray arrived. I hate that woman with all that I am. Worse still, Ian has not been the same since she walked through the castle doors. Cook says she is visiting for only a short time, but any time is too long. I must not fear, for surely Ian would not like a woman of such loose moral standing. I heard the reason she is at Braemar is because she fell in love with a footman, and her father is desperate to find a wealthy suitor for her to marry. Tonight I meet with the others, and Elsa will know what to do.

May 24, 1786

The spell did not work. He is as smitten with her as he had been from the start. If there were a way to use her as part of the ceremony, I would do so. Yet I fear due to her status, her absence would not go unnoticed.

My stomach clenched. Was she talking about a sacrifice when she spoke of the ceremony? Is that what I had seen in my dream? Could it be that they actually did kill people? And what was this about spells?

May 28, 1786

I saw them kiss in the north meadow today. I was out gathering berries when I heard their laughter. She in her expensive gown of gold silk. What does he find so fascinating about her? She is not so beautiful. I wish she would leave soon. I have heard Cook say her parents plan to take her to London for a month, and their departure cannot come soon enough for me.

As I continued reading, the entries sounded more desperate and talk of "the others" more frequent. Even as I read back over the entries, I still couldn't see where the relationship between Ian and Laria had gone beyond friendship. It sounded more like a crush or flirtation. My heart missed a beat when Laria made mention of a love spell again, and in the margins she listed several herbs and one or two items I couldn't even pronounce.

June 2, 1786

Margot is ill. I cannot imagine what made her sick so suddenly.

The short entry made the hair on my arms stand on end. Laria had tried poisoning Margot? I could almost envision Laria writing those words, a smug smile on her lips.

The bedroom light flickered, as did the lamp on my nightstand. The air around me turned colder, a mist developed, and a figure slowly emerged.

Here we go again, I thought to myself, steadying for Laria's arrival.

The journal slipped from my fingers.

It wasn't Laria. It was my mom.

She looked beautiful, younger than I remembered; her skin soft and so smooth. She wore a white flowing gown and looked like an angel.

"Mom," I said, the single word little more than a whisper. I stared at her, taking in features I had long forgotten about. Since her death, I had refused to look at pictures of her since it made me too depressed. But the way she looked now reminded me of a photo that had been taken shortly after she'd met my dad when they were college students. The picture had been taken at a senior camping trip to Lake Shasta, California. It was my favorite photo—one Dad kept on a shelf in his office.

"You must not trust Ian MacKinnon, Riley," she said, her voice intense, almost cold.

"What?" I said, stunned at what I was hearing. "Ian is my friend."

"Hear me well—he is not who he says he is. He is dangerous and you must stay away from him."

I opened my mouth and she disappeared, just like that. Gone as fast as she'd come.

Tears burned my eyes. "Mom?" I said, the single word coming out as a croak.

Nothing but silence.

What the hell?

I bit the inside of my lip until I tasted blood. Why would she come now only to tell me not to trust Ian?

With anger, sadness, and confusion consuming me, I went to my dresser drawer, ripped it open, and found the pair of red socks where I kept my razor blades.

I thought of the promise I'd made to Shane. Of the promise I'd made to myself, and Ian too. He had told me I was strong...but I didn't feel strong, especially now.

I yanked the socks from the drawer, pulled the matchbox out, and tossed the socks aside.

Just one small cut, I reasoned, walking into the bathroom and locking the door behind me.

Chapter Twenty-Two

Something tickled my nose, and I brushed at it with the back of my hand.

The tickling continued.

Slowly opening my eyes, I found myself looking into intense blue eyes, framed by long, thick lashes. My heart gave a jolt. Ian lay beside me, a devilish grin on his handsome face and a feather in his long-fingered hand.

I smiled as I stared into his amazing eyes—until the memory of my mom's visit came back with a vengeance. I had cried myself to sleep after she'd appeared and then vanished just as quickly. Too many emotions still raced through me. I couldn't understand why, after all this time, she had finally come to me...only to drop a bombshell and tell me not to trust Ian. Did I have this all wrong? Was Ian really who he said he was or had I fallen in love with a dark spirit?

Ian's smile faltered and his hand dropped to the comforter, the feather forgotten. "What's wrong, Riley?"

I swallowed past the lump in my throat. "My mom came to visit."

His eyes narrowed. "Your mom? Did you have another séance with Miss Akin and Anne Marie?"

"No, I was reading the journal and my mom appeared before my eyes."

He immediately looked skeptical. I didn't need skepticism right now. It had been a year since I'd seen her and why had she come now? Was it because she felt I was in danger?

"What did she say?"

I sat up, brought my knees to my chest. He sat up, too, very slowly, watching me closely. I knew I couldn't read his mind, but I could read his face. He was hesitant, unsure of what to say to me.

The question was why?

And what about the dream I'd had the other night with the cloaked figures, particularly the figure who had tried to kill me. It *had* been Ian.

Perhaps that dream had been a warning from my mother, instead of Laria trying to brainwash me into believing Ian was fooling me. I was so confused.

"Riley, do you trust me?" Ian's voice was calm and matter-of-fact. I'd never seen him look so serious...or worried.

I wanted to trust him more than I'd ever wanted anything.

And yet, how could I ignore my mother's warning? Why else would she come to me now, unless I really was in danger?

I saw the pain in Ian's eyes as I hesitated answering him, but I wouldn't lie. In fact, I knew he could read my thoughts, so he didn't even need to hear it from me.

"I swear to you, everything I have said is the honest-to-God truth, Riley. I have no need to lie to you. You are my friend, and I tell you now that the spirit you saw was not your mother. I am sure of it."

I rolled off the bed, crossed my arms over my chest. "It *was* my mom, Ian. I saw her with my own eyes!"

He pressed his palms together and sighed heavily, tapping his index fingers against his lips.

I thought of the nightmare, of the horror I had felt surrounded by those cloaked figures. I wanted Ian to see exactly what I had seen, to feel what I felt, so I grabbed his hands. "Explain this," I said, pushing the creepy dream at him.

When he saw himself cloaked and holding the knife up, ready to plunge it into my chest, he flinched.

Then his arms were around me, pulling me close. "I swear on my mother's soul I would never hurt you," he whispered against my forehead. "Laria is sending you those dreams and thoughts in order to turn you against me. That's what she wants more than anything. I believe it was she who came to you earlier in your mother's form."

Which meant my mom really hadn't come to me. I wanted to scream my rage at the top of my lungs.

"I know you want to believe it was her, but you must trust me in this."

I knew from experience that Laria would stop at nothing to keep me from helping Ian pass over—even come to me as my mom.

What a cruel, twisted bitch.

I settled against him, burying my face in the crook between his shoulder and neck. His hands moved up and down my back, coming to rest at my hip, and he kissed my forehead. He made me feel cherished and loved, and I feared losing these moments.

"You must do something for me," he whispered.

I swallowed hard, terrified of what he was about to ask. "I'll try."

"When your mum comes to you again and shows herself, ask her a question only the two of you would know the answer to. See what her response is. If she can answer you truthfully, then you have cause to believe it is she. If she cannot answer you, then it isn't her. But you must be sure to keep the answer from your mind at all times, so she cannot read your thoughts and guess the correct answer."

He lifted my chin as he stared at me. "If I could, I would bring your mom to you, you know that, don't you?"

Touched that he was so concerned, I nodded and managed a smile. I felt exhausted from lack of sleep and from constantly being on edge. My mom's sudden appearance had been the final straw.

"Will you stay with me for a while?" I asked, desperate to feel his arms around me as I slept.

"Of course," he said, looking relieved by the request.

"Don't go anywhere. I need to wash my face and brush my teeth."

He nodded, and sat back down on the bed. "I'll be right here."

In the bathroom, I turned on the faucet. Cupping my hands beneath the cool water, I started splashing water on my face. The matchbox with the razor blades inside sat in the bottom of the wastebasket. I hadn't cut earlier, and instead had thrown the blades away, but the urge to cut still pulled at me. Would I always have this urge? I wondered. Would I be like an alcoholic constantly fighting the desire to drink?

I had promised too many people I would stop, and I needed to move forward with my life. Cutting was only holding me back. I reached for a towel, wiped off my face, and looked into the mirror. I instantly noticed something odd—a dark spot near my pupil, and as I leaned in, the green irises were turning a dark brown...and my blonde hair was turning brown.

Icy fear slid along my spine.

Laria's face stared back at me, transposed over mine. The corners of her mouth lifted in a wicked smile that chilled me to the bone, but I tried hard not to react. She had messed with me for too long, and had gone too far when she'd manifested as my mom.

"Stop it," I whispered, but the image didn't fade.

I put my hands over my eyes. "Leave me alone, Laria."

Her laughter rushed through me, all around me, so loud I nearly screamed.

"Riley?" Ian walked straight through the bathroom door, his expression intense as his arms came around me, hugging me from behind.

Laria's energy was still with us but fading fast. I heard a sound, and Ian must have heard it too, because he straightened and put me at arm's length.

The tune started soft, familiar, but not in a good way, and then I heard the chant from my nightmare. "Do you hear it?" I asked, my fingers gripping his arms.

He nodded. With a resigned sigh, he released me and stepped back into my bedroom. I was right on his heels.

"Be gone, Laria," he said wearily. "Leave Riley and her family alone. This is our war, not hers."

The chanting stopped immediately.

"What really happened between the two of you?" I asked, the question eating at me since reading the journal and finding nothing that alluded to anything more than a crush. "I mean, what kind of a relationship did you have for her to go so ballistic? Were you lovers?"

"No. She was a servant and a friend, but nothing more. God's truth, I never touched her, Riley. Ever. Not even a kiss."

The words hadn't left his mouth when the glass on my bedside table flew toward me. The glass shattered against the door, landing in a thousand pieces onto the wood floor. If Ian hadn't have pushed me out of the way, it would have hit me, maybe even killed me since the bottom was so thick and heavy.

I heard a startled yelp from downstairs, and then footsteps headed my way. "Riley," Miss Akin yelled, knocking on the door. She sounded winded. "Are you alright, my dear?"

"Yeah, I'm okay, Miss A. I just tripped on the rug and the glass flew out of my hand."

"It sounded like it hit the wall."

"The door, actually. Sorry, it slipped from my fingers."

The door started to open, but I stopped it with my foot. "There's glass everywhere, and I don't want you stepping on the shards. I'll take care of it. Can you get the broom and dustpan for me?"

"Of course, my dear. Don't you move, and be careful not to cut yourself. I'll be back in a jiff."

A second later I heard her heading down the stairs.

Ian stood behind me, and he was touching my hair. Despite the fact I had a maniac ghost trying to kill me, I couldn't deny the pleasure that rushed through me at such a simple touch. He was the only sanity in my otherwise crazy-ass world.

"She's coming back," I said, bending over and picking up the big pieces of glass on the floor.

He went down on his haunches beside me.

"Don't waste your energy helping me," I said, wanting him to stay with me tonight. I needed his companionship and his strength, especially with Laria becoming so aggressive.

"Just pretend I'm not here."

Easier said than done, I thought, as Miss Akin tapped on the door.

I opened the door and she stepped into the room with broom and dustpan in hand. "*Tsk, tsk.* You have bare feet, girl. What are you thinking? Go sit down and get off the floor before you cut your feet."

I did as she asked and sat down on the edge of the bed while she cleaned up. "You need to be more careful. You gave me such a fright—I nearly had a heart attack thinking it was that Laria character." She gave a shiver. "It sounded like that glass hit the wall with force. It would have packed quite a punch had it hit you instead."

"A good thing it didn't then," I said, feeling Ian lay on the bed behind me. The bed shifted slightly, and I watched Miss Akin closely to see if she'd noticed, but apparently she hadn't.

Ian touched my back, drawing a lazy finger along my spine. Gooseflesh rose all over my body. He wrote a letter, then another, and I quickly realized he was spelling my name. I wanted to turn and smile, or say my name aloud, but I didn't want to let on to Miss Akin that he was with us.

"Are you alright, love?" Miss Akin asked, glancing at me in a strange way.

"Yes, I'm fine." Even my voice sounded funny. Huskier.

She walked into the bathroom, and a second later I heard the pieces of glass hit the wastebasket. My stomach tightened knowing the blades were in the matchbox. I so didn't need an intervention right now.

I breathed a silent sigh of relief when she returned with a wet towel and wiped the floor with it. "You've been so quiet these past few days, I was beginning to worry about you. Worried that Laria isn't leaving you alone."

"I've just been hanging out and talking on the phone with friends."

"So...are you any closer to helping the young MacKinnon?"

"I think so."

"I think you must do so quickly," she said, her voice intense. "My intuition tells me that sooner versus later is the best route to take. Does that make sense?"

I nodded, and behind me Ian went very still.

"Remember, Anne Marie will assist you if she can."

"I know." She dried the floor and stood. "I know you know this, Riley...but just remember, dear, that he is not of this world any longer."

I wondered if Anne Marie hadn't been able to read me like a book during my visit to her house and reported back to Miss A. That, or maybe Miss Akin's intuition was right on the money. Whatever the case might be, I wanted her to stop talking right now, to warn her that the guy she was talking about was right behind me, listening to every word.

"And he deserves to spend eternity in the next life, wherever that might be. It wouldn't be fair to keep him here with you, no matter how much you like him."

I swallowed past the lump that had mysteriously formed in my throat. Talk about ruining the moment.

"Well, I've said enough about the matter. I can tell you are tired, so I shall let you get your rest, my dear."

She closed the door behind her, and Ian pulled me toward him and rested his chin on the top of my head. I already missed him.

Damn, why was life so unfair?

I waited until Miss Akin's steps faded before I said, "Will you do me a favor?"

He pulled away. "Of course."

"Will you sit for me while I draw you?"

The corners of his mouth lifted, making my heart clench. "Yes, of course. I'd be honored."

Chapter Twenty-Three

I sat in the chair near my bedroom window staring at the drawing of Ian. I had to admit—it was pretty damn good. I caught the angles of his gorgeous face...the high cheekbones, sensual lips...and those intense eyes that mirrored love and desire.

The same love and desire I felt for him.

It had been an incredible hour where I could stare at him without feeling awkward or self-conscious, and he had sat there so quietly, just watching me in return. I wished I knew what he was thinking, and wondered if he could read my scorching thoughts.

Oddly, I didn't care if he could read me. The sexual energy had been charged, and unfortunately, he had faded and disappeared before we could do anything about it.

I smiled and set the drawing down, and picked up Laria's journal. If it wasn't for Laria, I'd feel no urgency in helping Ian pass over right now. I thought about what Miss Akin had said. She had reminded me that what I had with Ian was impossible, that helping him had to come first and that we could have no future.

But it was tough to remember that when I was looking into his beautiful blue eyes.

Frustrated, I flipped to the page of the journal where I'd left off when my mother, or Laria, had made her appearance.

I unconsciously rubbed at the scar that had formed on my leg from where I'd cut myself the day I'd met Ian. Every single time I thought of my mother, or actually *Laria's* visit, I felt the familiar temptation to cut.

If it wasn't for the fact I hated the aftereffects of drinking, I'd probably get hammered, but I wasn't a pretty drunk, and drugs weren't an option, especially given the fact Laria might come through...and I can't imagine how freaked out that would make me.

The desire to get my razor ate at me, making me wonder if the darkness of Laria's spirit wasn't coming through to me in different ways.

Refocusing, I took a deep breath and started reading.

June 20, 1786

I overheard Lady MacKinnon talking about Ian and Margot this morning. She said they would make a good match and positively glows every time Margot comes about. He cannot marry her. He cannot marry anyone else. Tonight I will visit with the elders. Another spell is in order, but this time I will take no chances. She must go.

June 22, 1786

I have everything I need, but I do not know if I will have to go through with it. I caught him staring at me today during dinner. Even Laird MacKinnon's valet was irritated by the attention Ian paid me this evening.

June 27, 1786

I hate him. I hate him with everything I possess. He will pay for what he has done.

It was the final entry written in a shaky scrawl.

I frowned. What was I missing? Why had Maggie wanted me to read this journal, if not to find the answers on how to help Ian?

I started at page one again, flipped through each page, and skimmed each passage twice.

A breeze blew through the room.

My heart jolted. My mom stood before me, wearing the same white gown as before, but this time she was more of a fine mist than a solid form.

It was hard to remember that this wasn't my mom, despite the fact she looked just like her. I couldn't let on that I knew it was Laria.

"Have you told Ian you do not trust him and want him out of your life?" she asked.

"I'm working on it." I set the journal aside, cleared my throat. "Will you answer a question?"

"Of course." Though she smiled, I could hear the hesitation in her voice.

"What was the name of the song you sang to me at bedtime when I was a little girl?"

Her eyes narrowed. "Do you test me, Riley?"

Fear and apprehension crept up my spine. "No...I just forgot the name of the song, that's all."

Just in case she tried to read my thoughts, I focused on another song, literally singing the lyrics in my mind.

"I'm a little teapot," she blurted, looking pleased with herself.

It had been the very song I'd been thinking of. A song I hated from the time I tried to play it on the piano and my piano teacher had snapped a ruler over my knuckles when I couldn't get the notes right.

"Why did you really kill him, Laria? Was it because he didn't like you as much as you liked him?"

Though she tried to keep her expression blank, I could see anger brimming in her eyes. My mom never looked that sinister when she was mad. Ever. Her gaze shifted briefly to the journal in my hands. "What are you talking about?"

I clearly heard her Scottish brogue creeping in this time.

"I know who you are," I said, digging deep for a strength I doubted I possessed.

Her eyes widened. "I am your mother, Riley."

"You are *not* my mother, Laria."

As I continued to stare at her, I saw my mother's features fade. The blue eyes turned dark brown, and her hair changed from blonde to Laria's now familiar long brown locks.

"Why did you kill him?" I asked again.

Laria looked horrible—paler than usual, with deeper, darker hollows beneath her eyes. "Because he deserved to die after what he did to me."

"And what did he do to you, exactly?"

"He made me believe he would marry me."

"He never asked you to marry him, and he never touched you."

"You know nothing about me or Ian for that matter. He *did* care for me. He desired me. He *loved* me!" she said between clenched teeth.

"And so you killed him because you felt he betrayed you? Why did you feel it necessary to curse him as well? Wasn't murder enough?"

I could see the fury in her face and hear it in her voice. "If you help him, I swear I shall make you pay for all eternity."

"What does that mean? You'll kill me and curse me as well?" I had no doubt she'd do just that, and the very idea of being an earth-bound spirit was frightening.

"Perhaps," she said, looking like she'd love to kill me right that second. The wicked smile that tugged at her lips made my blood turn cold.

"Do you think I fear dying?"

"No, you don't fear death...because you should have died in your mum's place."

A fist to the gut would have had the same impact as her cruel words.

"You are the reason she is not here with you and your family. And now because of you, your brother no longer has a mother, and your father no longer has a wife. You wonder why she doesn't come to you when other spirits can, and yet you know deep down it's be-cause you killed her. She resents you for taking her away from your father and your brother."

Was Laria right? Did my mom stay away because she blamed me for her death?

I ran a trembling hand down my face. "Shut up, Laria."

She floated toward me, her feet inches from the floor. I dug my nails into my palms. She looked at my fisted hands and smiled. "You like to hurt yourself, do you not, Riley? In fact, you yearn to hurt yourself now. To take away the pain you feel inside. I understand why."

"Leave me alone, Laria. Just go away."

"I will never leave you alone. Unless you forget about Ian

MacKinnon. Forget about him, Riley, and I shall leave you and your family in peace."

Peace. I'd never have peace if I turned my back on Ian. "No," I said, tired of her threats.

She slammed me up against the wall, knocking the breath from me. She brought her face inches from mine. I could see the cruelty in her dark eyes, the hatred she felt toward me, and it chilled me to the bone.

"Forget him, Riley. He is not your concern."

Her ice-cold fingers encircled my neck, and I clawed at her hands.

"Forget him and live, Riley," she whispered in my ear. "If you help him, I shall kill you...and those you love."

A second later she disappeared and I fell onto the floor, my hand at my throat.

I rushed toward the wastebasket only to find it empty. Shit! Miss Akin must have emptied it.

I looked for anything sharp. The nail that held my calendar on the wall would work.

My heart pounded against my chest, sweat forming on my brow. I crossed the room, pulled the nail from the wall, and headed for the bathroom to clean it with rubbing alcohol.

That's when I saw the drawing of Ian on the floor, and it was as effective as having a cold glass of water thrown in my face.

Chapter Twenty-Four

I stood with Megan at the glen, and I was seriously buzzed. Drinking more than one beer hadn't been the smartest thing to do, but it beat cutting, and I needed something to dull the pain and anxiety that had been coursing through me since Laria had masqueraded as my mom.

"Look who's here," Megan said, motioning to the familiar Peugeot that pulled into the glen. Johan and three of his friends poured out of the car. "Milo told him that you weren't looking for a boyfriend, so I think he'll leave you alone."

Apparently he'd gotten the message loud and clear because he glanced my way, lifted a brow, and quickly turned away.

Typical man-whore behavior.

Megan nudged me and nodded toward Cassandra, who was making out with, of all people, Tom. *Eww!!* I could barely stomach the sight. What was she thinking?

I glanced over at Johan, who by his expression seemed as surprised as everyone by Cassandra's sudden interest in Tom, and maybe even a little jealous. It was funny how guys reacted when the shoe was suddenly on the other foot.

"Hey."

I jumped at the sound of Shane's voice from behind me.

Apparently Shane had started seeing Joni, the emo girl who had been at Milo's party. No wonder he'd been MIA the past week or so.

Despite the fact I was the last one to find out about his relationship, I was happy for him. He'd never really had a girlfriend, and I could tell by the girls' reaction to his California skater boy good looks at registration that he was going to be popular.

"I haven't talked to you for a while. Are you doing okay?" he asked, shoving his hands in his jeans pockets.

"Yeah," I lied. "What about you? You haven't been home that much."

"I got a call from the school's football coach today." I could hear the excitement in his voice. "He's interested in having me try out for the team."

"That's awesome, Shane." He'd loved playing soccer, or what they called football in the U.K., before our mom died, and he was known for his speed and scoring ability. I remembered spending long days at the field cheering him on, and I looked forward to doing it again.

It was then I noticed the dark circles under his eyes. "You look a little tired. Is everything okay?"

He shrugged. "I haven't slept all that great. I've been having some crazy-ass dreams lately."

My pulse skittered. "Like what?"

"Like I'm being hunted by someone—or something. When I try to wake up, I can't. When I do wake, it's like I can't breathe, like someone is sitting on my chest. That's why I've been staying with Richie. I thought maybe it was the inn—you know, with it being old and all, but it doesn't seem to matter where I'm at. I just always feel like there's someone stalking me."

Laria was getting to Shane. I had known it at Milo's party because I'd seen it for myself, but I hadn't realized it had continued. After our last encounter, she would be even more relentless.

"I sound mental, don't I?" he asked, one side of his mouth lifting.

"Not really." I nudged his arm. "Things will get better, you just wait and see. And maybe lay off the pot, especially now that you're getting back into soccer."

His lips quirked and he glanced across the fire at Joni. "Actually, I haven't smoked for a few days."

I was glad to hear it. Nothing good would come of it...just like my getting shit-faced wouldn't help me—or cutting, for that matter.

Joni smiled and waved at us. I grinned and waved back...but the grin slid from my lips a second later. Standing right behind her was Laria. She wore a creepy black robe. The hood was up, but her features were clearly visible, especially her dark, menacing eyes and malicious smile.

She leaned down and touched Joni's face in a slow caress.

Joni didn't flinch or react at all, which made me wonder if maybe Shane was sensitive to spirits.

Laria started skipping toward me, in a slow, disjointed kind of way—an eerie dance that made my insides churn. The chanting I'd heard in my dream and the other night when Ian was over began.

It was all I could do not to slap my hands over my ears.

"I think we should go," I said, watching with dread the closer she came.

Laria's fingers brushed through Shane's hair, then over my shoulder.

Shane grabbed my arm. "Come on, I'll have Joni's sister drop us off."

"You're dead," the chilling voice said in my ear.

After hurling the entire contents of my stomach into the toilet, I crashed out and fell into a fitful sleep, and had a dream about Laria.

She was writing in the journal, but this time I saw her peel back the edges of the binding, and write something there. Whatever it was, she constantly looked over her shoulder, toward the door, like she was terrified of being caught. Someone called out to her. Looking nervous, she quickly slid the journal back in its hiding place under the cot, and seconds later a man appeared at her door.

The vision faded and I woke up.

I turned on the lamp next to my bed, and reached for the journal I had stashed in the drawer of my nightstand.

Excited, I flipped to the last page and slowly began to peel it back. My hand shook as the paper ripped beneath my fingers. Taking a steadying breath, I took my time, and my stomach tightened seeing a now familiar scrawl appear.

It was Laria's writing and it said:

To this land you were born and to this land you shall die, and for all eternity you will roam its borders and not beyond.

In the margin was a list of ingredients, and I had a feeling it was the concoction she had used to kill Ian. Beside it was a phrase written in what I assumed to be Gaelic, an old Celtic language. I couldn't pronounce the words, and honestly, I was too afraid to, terrified I would make matters worse. I had a new appreciation for the "other side" now, for things most people couldn't see or explain. The power the dead could have over the living was mind-boggling.

Cold air enveloped me, and I fought a shiver as it rushed along my spine at the same time I felt someone standing nearby. Though I was seriously tempted, I didn't look over my shoulder, but I did glance at the mirror on the back of my bathroom door. I could just make out a figure. Laria's reflection stared back at me. She meant to scare me...and was doing a damn good job of it.

I wanted to run screaming from the room, but instead I calmly said, "Begone all evil spirits."

She was still there. I expected her cruel laughter, but instead she made no sound and floated to the foot of the bed, where she stopped and stared at me.

Her gaze shifted from me to the journal in my hand.

I shoved the journal under my pillow and scrambled off the bed. In the blink of an eye, she was standing right beside me. She was a couple of inches taller than me and her form was almost solid. The lights flickered in my room, and I knew she was sucking up all the energy she possibly could.

"Go away," I said, lifting my chin.

Her lips curved in a smile that didn't begin to touch her eyes. "Never."

"Leave me alone," I said with more force.

"I will kill those you love if you continue."

Though her words terrified me, I was tired of her threats. I was tired of her. "Leave here. Move on. You are not wanted or welcome here."

I think she was angry I wasn't showing fear. She had bullied me for so long, and now I had grown exhausted by her manipulation. Tired of the fear I felt on a daily basis. Tired of what she'd put Ian through. Tired of what she was doing to Shane, Anne Marie, and Miss Akin. Hell, for all I knew my dad could be affected too.

"I will haunt you for the rest of your days," she taunted.

"No, you won't."

She flinched as though I'd slapped her.

"I've read the journal, Laria. I know the curse."

"Do you think you have the power to end it?" she asked, her voice tinged with disbelief. "A curse *I* made."

I honestly didn't know the answer to that question, but I was going to find out...tonight.

The light above me crackled and popped, and I could hear the bulb shatter inside the fixture. Next, the light on my nightstand began to dim. "You're losing energy," I said with a calm that surprised me.

The lamp bulb popped, followed by the light in the bathroom. I heard a crack from the hallway and knew she was draining every resource.

Ian appeared behind her and I breathed a sigh of relief. She was thrust against the wall...all without him touching her. His gaze shifted up the wall, and Laria followed the route...up toward the ceiling.

He was doing to her what she had done to me.

And she didn't like it.

She was on the ceiling and she hung there, her long hair falling like an eerie curtain. I saw the look in her eyes, and I was surprised to see fear.

She made a horrific growling noise, and then she disappeared.

I went into Ian's arms and he held me tight, kissing my forehead.

I looked up into his eyes, smiled, and said, "I found it, Ian."

Chapter Twenty-Five

The castle's dining room was dark and eerie. Even though I had Ian with me, I felt nothing but overwhelming sadness. Sadness that soon he would be gone and I would have to start living my life without him.

I knew I should look at the positive and be happy Ian would finally have peace after roaming Braemar for the past two hundred years, but the future seemed impossibly gloomy.

Oddly, it kind of felt like going through a death. Like losing my mom all over again, and yet, this time it was different. Different in that I had control over the situation. I didn't have control over what had happened with my mom. I knew that, and despite what Laria had said about her death being my fault and her resenting me, I couldn't blame myself any longer. In my mind, I could right a wrong by helping Ian pass over and find peace.

Maybe his passing over would give us *all* peace.

Outside the weather raged, the wind whipped the branches, and rain pelted the windows. It was going to be a miserable night and I was already soaked to the skin.

"Are you ready?" I asked Ian, who had been quiet since we'd left the inn.

I had been surprised by the power he had shown over Laria, and I wondered how it had really been for these enemies to live in the afterlife together for over two centuries.

He nodded. "I am."

I pulled the drapes closed and turned on my flashlight. "What are you feeling?" I asked, needing to hear his thoughts.

His brows lifted. "I am excited to see my family, but I am also afraid of leaving here. This is all I have known."

"But you'll be free."

"True," he said, his hand brushing over the table in front of him. "And as exciting as that is, I am afraid of leaving you."

My heart squeezed with the love I felt for him. He was beautiful inside and out, and I feared I would never meet another man like him. My throat grew tight as I stared at him, memorizing every detail for later when he was gone. Thank God I had taken the time to draw the picture of him.

"Come here," he said softly, lifting his hand out to me.

I slid the backpack from my shoulder, letting it fall to the ground beside me.

I took his hand and he pulled me onto his lap, his arms encircling me, holding me tight. I slid my arms around his neck, buried my face in his hair, and inhaled deeply.

"I miss you already," I said, not bothering to wipe the tears that slid down my cheeks.

He released a breath but didn't respond, and I wondered, if like me, he didn't want to let go. Didn't want to say goodbye.

Ian held me tighter, and looked up at me, his eyes bright in the dark room. "You are so special, Riley. Do not ever forget that."

Why couldn't I have waited just one more night? Instead I had let Laria's threats get to me. *That time just wasn't now. I made a huge mistake. I don't want you to go yet.* The words were on the tip of my tongue.

He kissed me, his lips gentle and hard all at once. I felt his urgency, the raw need, and I kissed him in return, not holding anything back.

I wished we had made love...but I know if we had, it would have made leaving even harder than it already would be.

Minutes later, I cupped his face with my hands. "I'll never forget you," I whispered against his lips.

I was surprised to see tears in his eyes. "I'll always be with you. Always. Never forget that."

Unable to say anything for fear of bursting into tears, I nodded.

I went to get up, but he grabbed both my arms. "I love you, Riley."

My heart jumped at the declaration. I thought of these past weeks and how special he had made me feel, at how alive I felt because of him. "I love you, too, Ian."

He smiled softly, exposing those incredible deep dimples of his. "Remember, I will be closer than you think."

If only.

Once he passed over, I'd never see him again. Just like I'd never see my mom again.

"You must have faith, Riley."

"It's hard to have faith given what I know about the afterlife."

"Believe it or not, you have only scratched the surface of what is possible. You must believe in your heart that we will see each other again. Will you do that for me? Will you believe we will be together again?"

I forced a smile I didn't feel. "I'll believe we'll be together again one day...and I can hardly wait."

"Good girl," he said with a wink.

I kissed him one more time and stood on wobbly legs. No matter how much I wanted to keep Ian with me, I had to get in and out of there as fast as I could.

The room grew colder by the second, and I sensed a dark presence. I knew Ian felt it too, because he stood and moved closer to me.

"Stay in the chair," I said, and he sat back down, though reluctantly, his gaze all the while scanning the room.

Unzipping my backpack, I removed the parchment, the candles, and the lighter I'd brought with me. I took a deep breath. "Ready?"

He nodded.

Recalling the instructions I'd read in one of the books Anne Marie had given me, I lit the first candle, closed my eyes, and thought of my body being surrounded and filled with the white light. "I ask for light and happiness to fill this dwelling and those within it. Let all the binds that once tied, break. Remove all these ties and return to what once was. I release all those that are bound here to be free."

Next, I poured the salt and herbs around Ian and the entire table, not wanting Laria to get to either of us. The hair on my arms stood on end because I felt her watching—felt her anger, her intense hatred for both Ian and me. With trembling hand, I lit the gold candle and set it in the center of the table.

I closed my eyes again and envisioned what I wanted—for Ian to be released from Laria's spell, and for them both to move on...and for me and my family to have some much-needed peace.

A scream pierced the quiet and I was terrified to open my eyes... but I did. As expected, Laria stood before me, her feet not touching the floor, her hair floating all around her. She meant to scare me, meant to have me run away, but I straightened my shoulders and lifted my chin.

Ian stood but I held up my hand and shook my head. He didn't sit down, but he didn't move out of the circle either.

I continued. "White light protect us from all evil. Let only good energy remain in this place and return evil to where it came from."

Laria's forced laughter radiated up to the high ceiling, and I could feel her try to use her power to pull me from the circle. My entire body trembled with the effort it took to stay put. The herbs and salt worked a little, but I felt the spirits of Ian's family with us, giving us their energy.

"I am the only one who can release him," Laria screamed. "Don't you know that, you fool?" She lifted her head and I felt my feet leave the floor.

"Riley, don't let her control you," Ian said.

I focused my attention on staying put, and my feet once again touched solid ground.

Laria turned to Ian and with a jerk of her hand, he went flying across the room, his back hitting the solid wall with a thud. He had left the safety of the circle, and I feared the curse wouldn't work because of it.

He came right back at her, a complete blur. Seconds later he had her pinned against the opposite wall, his hands at her throat. "You are pure evil, Laria. Leave this place once and for all. Go to hell where you belong."

Laria clawed at him and he finally released her. Her chest rose and fell heavily, and she turned to me with such a wicked expression on her face, I steadied myself for what was to come.

With trembling hand, I lifted the candle and looked Laria in the eye. "Remove the evil spirit from my midst."

She rushed toward me, tackled me, and straddling my waist, started choking me. The candle had slipped from my hand and the light blew out, but I could still see the whites of her cruel eyes.

She was ripped off of me a moment later and slammed against the wall. A picture fell on top of her, and she pushed it aside, coming quickly to her feet.

She rushed me, but Ian caught her.

"Remove the evil spirit from our midst," I said again with more force. "Return her to where she belongs, and let all curses and spells die with her."

A man walked through the wall, straight toward us. I recognized him from my vision the night before. It was the man who had appeared at Laria's door. The man she'd hidden the journal from.

Laria looked at the man and shook her head.

He reached out, grabbed her wrist. She tried to pull away from his beefy hand, but he held her tight.

"You shall pay for this," she said, glaring at me.

"You have no power over me anymore," I said, feeling stronger by the second.

I saw the fear in her eyes fade, and for an instant I saw the girl she must have been when she'd been alive. She looked innocent—this woman who had haunted me since I'd arrived in Braemar.

The man glanced at me and then they faded before my eyes.

Laria was gone.

Elated, I looked to where Ian stood, and my stomach fell to my toes. He was so bright, nearly blinding, and fading fast. "No!" I said, but it was too late.

Before I could blink, he was gone.

Peace and tranquility filled the room, but inside I mourned the loss of my friend. Feeling like the breath had been sucked from my lungs, I fell to my knees, and tears slipped down my cheeks and onto the floor.

I brushed at the salt and herbs on the floor and winced as a sliver jabbed into my finger, but I welcomed the pain. A sob tore from my throat as I sat back on my heels and looked up at the picture of Maggie. The panic I felt waned under that smiling face, and as orbs floated toward me, dancing around me, a calm and peace I hadn't felt since my mom died settled deep within me.

Ian had gone home where he belonged, and I had helped him. I couldn't forget that even for a minute. This was a good thing. The right thing—and I had to get on with living my life without him. I stood, spent a few minutes brushing the salt and herbs under the rug, and grabbed each of the candles, putting them into the backpack.

I slid on my backpack and walked toward the staircase, filled with so many mixed emotions.

Brushing away tears, I looked over my shoulder one last time at the chair where Ian had been sitting. I touched my lips, remembering that last kiss.

"I'll never forget you," I said, and walked out the door.

Chapter Twenty-Six

I didn't get out of bed for four days. I convinced my dad and Miss Akin that I had the flu, but I think Miss A had guessed the truth. She had asked a few times about Ian, but I cried at the mention of his name. And she would in turn bring me cookies and tell me everything would be okay.

But it wasn't okay and wouldn't be okay, because I had lost the man I loved and I would never see him again.

Despite what he said.

I missed Ian with a passion, and selfishly wished I had kept him here, even if it meant putting up with Laria for all eternity. Yes, I was happy I had helped him. Yes, I was happy he was with his family and no longer tormented by Laria, but none of that would change the fact I had lost my best friend.

Someone knocked on my door. I thought about pretending to be asleep, but decided against it. Given my luck, my dad would call the doctor, or a psychiatrist, if I kept ignoring everyone.

"Come in," I said, sitting up against the headboard, hoping I didn't look as horrible as I felt.

It was Shane. He stepped into the room and closed the door behind him. "How you doing?"

"I'm alright," I said, glad to see him looking better than ever.

He glanced at the closed drapes. "It's nice outside. You want to take a walk or something?"

I hid a smile. My little brother was worried about me. Though I didn't feel like going anywhere, I had a feeling he'd drag me kicking and screaming from my bed if I refused. "Sure, but let me take a shower first. It's been a few days."

"Please do," he said, laughing and looking relieved. "I'll be downstairs when you're ready. How about if I ask Miss A to make you a grilled cheese?"

Grilled cheese was one of my favorite comfort foods. "I'd like that. Thanks."

He was halfway out the door when I asked, "Have you had any more of those creepy dreams?"

He shook his head. "No, thank God."

Relieved to hear it, I smiled. "Good."

"I'll see you downstairs," he said, a wide smile on his face.

I took a quick shower, and dried off my body and hair with a towel. I slid on my terry cloth robe and brushed out my hair. I had to admit I felt better already.

I opened the bathroom door and stopped in my tracks. The brush slipped from my fingers, clattering onto the wood floor.

My mother stood in front of me, barely visible, a bright light outlining her form. She was dressed in a beautiful cream-colored gown.

I took a quick step back.

Was it really my mom, or had the curse failed?

"Do not be afraid, sweetheart."

Sweetheart. It had been so long since I'd heard that endearment.

I shifted on my feet. "Are...are you really my mom?"

She smiled softly. "Yes, Riley, I'm your mom."

"How come you didn't visit me before now?" I could hear the accusation in my voice.

"I crossed over right away. Time there isn't the same as it is here."

I remembered Ian telling me something similar.

"There is so much to do on the other side. So much to learn. You can't possibly imagine how beautiful it is." She smiled softly.

"I wish I could see it for myself."

"You will one day, but until then, you have much to do with your life."

"I thought you blamed me for the wreck," I blurted before I lost my nerve. "I thought that's why you didn't come to visit me."

She shook her head. "My death was not your fault, Riley. It was no one's fault. It was just my time to go. You have to let go of the guilt you've been carrying around and focus on the gifts you now have. You were meant to see lost souls for a reason, and you've already helped an earthbound spirit cross over. I'm so proud of you."

She knew about Ian?

"Your gift can help so many, and you can learn to control it. Do not fear your abilities."

"I don't know how to control it though."

"Continue to read and talk to others who have similar gifts...like your friend, Anne Marie, and Miss Akin too. Use them as mentors to help you. Reach out to others. Soon you will be able to turn your gift on and off like a light switch."

She began to flicker, and I could feel her energy waning.

"I must go now, sweetheart, but I'll be here whenever you need me. Just say my name and think of me. You might not be able to see me in my physical form, but I'll be here regardless. You'll feel me. Don't ever doubt that." She hugged me tight and I hugged her back, tears streaming down my cheeks with the emotions that raged within me.

I never wanted to let go.

"There is someone else who wants to see you." She turned, looked to her left.

My heart pounded loud in my ears.

I stepped into my bedroom and followed her gaze to find Ian. He was a dimly lit figure just like my mom, surrounded by a bright light, but I could still make out his handsome features.

I had to fight to catch my breath.

"I love you, Riley," my mom said, fading fast.

"I love you, too, Mom."

As my mom faded, Ian grew brighter and the light in my room flickered.

My insides twisted as I looked into his brilliant blue eyes.

"I never thought I'd see you again," I said, feeling breathless, taking the steps that separated us.

His lips curved into the unforgettable smile I saw in my dreams each night.

"I miss you," I said, before I could stop myself.

"I miss you, too."

He looked amazing. As beautiful as ever...and at peace. "What's it like? Are you happy?"

"It is incredible, Riley. You will not believe how beautiful the other side is or all the love. I cannot put it into words."

"I wish I could see it."

"You will...one day, when it is your time."

"I wish it was my time now." I seriously meant it. I'd go with him in a heartbeat.

"You have a long life to live, and so much to look forward to. As your mom mentioned, you have a gift, and you must use it, just as you used it to help me." He reached out, touched my face. "Plus, all you have to do is think of me and I'll be here."

"Then you'll be here all the time." I'd never leave my room. I'd want to be with him forever.

He laughed and my heart lurched at the sound. God, I missed that laugh.

"I love you," I said, before he disappeared.

He grinned—all deep dimples and white teeth. "I love you, too."

My stomach coiled as he started to fade fast. "Please don't go!"

"I'll be right here, Riley."

"How will I know you're here if I can't see you?"

"I'll leave signs."

"Signs? What kind of signs?"

"Scents, flowers, birds, poems, a song on the radio," he said with a wink. "You'll feel me, and know in your heart that it's me."

Then as fast as he'd come, he was gone.

True to Ian's word, he left me signs to let me know he was still around—one being a poem that fell from the book Anne Marie had lent to me about psychic mediums. I had been reading a chapter on tormented souls when out fell a handwritten poem called "A Red, Red Rose" by Robert Burns, a poet who had lived during Ian's time.

The following morning when I woke up, there was a red rose on my nightstand. I'd asked Miss Akin, Shane, and Dad about it, but all of them denied giving it to me. And this afternoon, while driving the highway to Aberdeen with Megan, the car radio had switched stations without us touching the dial, and "Wonderwall" was playing. I'd had to blink back tears.

"Sit down and I'll start your highlights," Megan said, drawing me back to the present. We were in my bedroom, and I sat on a chair with a plastic cape draped around my shoulders waiting to be *transformed*, as Megan put it. I just hoped she knew what she was doing. She said she colored hair all the time.

I didn't have anything to lose. I needed a change, and figured the start of school was the perfect time to make that change.

"I can't believe school starts on Tuesday. Where did the summer go?" Megan said, brushing out my hair.

I know exactly where my summer had gone. If I could relive every minute of it, I'd do so in a heartbeat.

"Hey, what are you doin' with a drawing of Kade MacKinnon?"

I followed her gaze to the drawing of Ian that sat beside the chair near the window. I'd been staring at it last night before I went to bed, and I had forgotten to put it away.

My pulse skittered. "Kade MacKinnon?" Kade MacKinnon looked like Ian?

"Yeah, that's him alright...uh, dressed like a pirate." Her eyes widened a bit, and she looked at me strangely.

What could I possibly say to get myself out of this one? I had drawn a picture of a guy I had presumably never met before. That wouldn't fly at all. "It's a MacKinnon ancestor who I saw in one of the books about the town."

"Wow, what a crazy resemblance," she said, apparently buying my story. "Oh and speaking of Kade, the MacKinnons' return tomorrow night."

"Yeah, they've been on vacation all summer, right?"

"They're on holiday," she said, correcting me.

"Right, on holiday," I repeated.

"Hopefully you can meet Cait before school starts. You'll like her. You'd never know she was filthy rich by the way she acts, or the way she dresses. She shops only at thrift marts. Very funky."

"She sounds like fun," I said, excited to meet them both.

Megan reached for a foil, and started to work on the highlights. "She's a year younger than us...and a bit of a rebel."

"A rebel, in what way?"

"She likes punk music and industrial rock, wears a lot of dark makeup. Kind of emo-ish, but not totally committed like Joni. Oh, and she dated Johan for a week or so, but Kade wasn't too keen about it, so they stopped going out."

"And what about Kade? What's he like?"

"He's—how do I say it, more reserved than his sister, but really cool. He's one of those people who treats everyone the same, no matter what. He doesn't always say a lot, but you get the idea that there's a lot going on behind those blue eyes."

My stomach tightened. Blue eyes? "Does he have a girlfriend?"

She shook her head. "No, and not because the girls haven't tried. I mean, he's dated here and there, but I've never heard anyone say a bad thing about him. Kade just never seemed that interested in any one girl. He plays a lot of football and that seems to be his focus."

I didn't want to set myself up for disappointment, but the more Megan talked about Kade MacKinnon, the more fired up I was to meet him.

Chapter Twenty-Seven

I knew Cait MacKinnon the minute she walked into the school cafeteria. The dark hair and large blue eyes were a dead giveaway. Megan had been right—she was a rebel, her clothing not new like everyone else's. Her shirt had a threadiness about it that any punk rocker would love, and the platinum chunks in her hair and the dark makeup set her apart from the norm.

I liked her immediately, and even better, we clicked instantly.

"So I hear Johan is into you," she said, lifting her brows high.

I felt my cheeks grow hot. "I don't think so. At least not anymore."

Cait rolled her eyes. "You were smart to kick his ass to the curb. He tries to sink his hook into everyone. He's such a bloody wanker."

Megan snorted, while Cassandra nodded in agreement. I noticed Cassandra seemed a lot less hostile around me, and was almost tolerable, though I had a feeling we would never be good friends.

"How do you like livin' at the inn?"

"It's a bit big and drafty...but it's growing on me."

She laughed. "I know the feeling."

"I bet," I said, realizing I'd have to be careful and not ever let on that I'd actually been inside her home.

"I can see the inn from my bedroom window. It's nice to see

lights on over there now. It was empty for so long."

"I can see the castle from my room, too," I said, feeling like an idiot the second I said it. Of course I could see the castle...if she could see the inn.

She grinned. "You'll have to come over sometime."

"I'd like that," I said, even though I wasn't sure I could handle being in the castle right now. Ian's departure had left a hole in my heart, and returning to the scene of said departure would be tough.

"Let's make plans." She slung her backpack on the table, unzipped the outer pocket, and rummaged through it. "Damn it, I left my money at home. I wonder if Kade has first lunch."

My heart skipped a beat at the mention of her brother. Megan met my gaze and winked, before popping a cracker into her mouth.

"I think he does have first lunch," Cassandra said, fussing with her hair. "I just passed him in the hall. In fact, there he is."

I followed Cassandra's gaze to the double doors.

My heart missed a beat. I could barely breathe.

Kade MacKinnon looked almost exactly like Ian. He was maybe an inch or two taller than Ian, and had the same broad shoulders but he was more muscular. His hair wasn't as long as Ian's, but it was layered and shaggy.

He sat down at a table, with, of all people, Johan and Tom.

Great.

"I'll be right back," Cait said, leaving her backpack and its contents strewn on the tabletop as she headed toward her brother.

Kade looked up as his sister approached and smiled. Oh my God, did he have dimples?

I set my sandwich down and took a drink of pop, unable to take my eyes off of Kade.

He stood, reached into his pocket and pulled out a few bills, and handed them to Cait. She smiled, said something to him, and walked back our way.

His gaze abruptly shifted to me.

My breath caught in my throat, and I felt like I'd been hit in the stomach. I'd know those long-lashed blue eyes anywhere. He stared at me for a moment, and then the sides of his mouth lifted. My stomach did a little flip. He did have dimples, deep dimples, just like Ian.

Despite my effort to play it cool, I grinned like an idiot.

Megan followed my gaze and turned back to me, brow arched. "You could play a little hard to get, you know?" she said, her lips twitching. "Didn't I tell you he was hot?"

Hot was an understatement. It was like looking at Ian. My Ian.

It was ridiculous to hope for something that couldn't be. So what...he looked just like Ian. Why wouldn't he? He was his descendant, after all.

"He's checking you out pretty hard," Megan said, dipping a spoon into her yogurt. "It's the highlights. I tell you, people have been complimenting me all day long."

I laughed under my breath, feeling giddy. "You did a great job," I said, feeling as light as air.

By the end of the day I was a little bummed. I'd hoped I'd have at least one class with Kade, or at the very least, pass him in the hall or on the stairs, but no such luck.

I did have Cait in two of my classes though and we exchanged cell numbers. I kept remembering how Megan said that she and her brother were nothing alike. I hoped I got to know them both well enough to see if that were true.

I met Megan near the parking lot. She stood with Milo and Shane, the latter looking really happy, if the wide smile on his face were to tell.

"I take it you had a good day?" I asked Shane.

"Yeah, it's definitely a bit different than I expected. I have to get a handle on the language. My art teacher has such a thick accent, I can hardly follow him."

"I know what you mean." I had the same situation in history where I caught about every third word the teacher said.

"Hey, there's a group heading over to the glen at four," Megan said, piping in. "You want to meet me there or I can drop by and pick you up? I just have to go home and tidy up my room first or my mum will have my head."

I nodded. "Sure, pick me up."

"I'll see you guys at the glen," Shane said, already rushing to catch up with Joni.

I smiled to myself, relieved that both of us were fitting in. Dad would be ecstatic.

As I walked across the grass, I glanced up at the hillside where I'd sat with Ian that day that seemed so long ago. In time, I wanted to go up there again and take my drawing pad—but it would take awhile. The memories were too raw. I would always remember the way Ian had rested his head in my lap, and how he'd pulled my head down for a kiss.

"Riley!"

I turned to find Cait and Kade walking toward me.

Excitement raced through me, and I tried hard not to stare at Kade, but it was tough. He looked so much like Ian.

"Hey," I said, self-consciously brushing a hand through my hair, hoping I didn't make matters worse.

"I wanted to introduce you to my brother," Cait said. "Kade, this is Riley. Riley, my brother Kade."

"Nice to meet you," I said, extending my hand.

He took my hand, his long fingers sliding over mine. His touch was electric, and I could only hope my cheeks weren't as hot as they felt.

"It's nice to meet you, Riley. I've heard a lot about you."

His voice was rich and the accent nice. "All good things, I hope."

"Of course," he said, with a grin that gave me butterflies in my stomach. Cait wandered off, leaving us alone, and we finally dropped hands.

"So, how was your vacation?" I asked, feeling nervous.

He seemed surprised I had known he'd been away for the summer. "It was nice, but if I had my way, I'd stay home."

"Spoken like someone who takes a lot of vacations," I said teasingly.

He laughed, the sound like music to my ears. "Don't get me wrong. I love going on holiday, but after a week or two I'm ready to come home."

I nodded in understanding.

"And what about you, Riley. Do you miss your home?"

I glanced past him to the small group of girls huddled near the fence, watching us. I could sense animosity all over them. "Yeah, I miss Portland...but I'm starting to like it here. Everyone has been really nice."

He bit his lip, much in the same way Ian had, running his upper teeth along that full lower lip. The mannerisms were similar, and his face was Ian's—but I had to remember he wasn't Ian.

"I'm glad you like Braemar and I'm glad you're here."

"Thanks," I said, happy with the comment. "I am, too."

"Would you like a ride home?" he asked, his expression saying he hoped I said yes.

Excitement raced through me. "That's okay. I don't live that far," I said, instantly regretting the words. Oh my God, why had I said that?

"What are you so afraid of?" he asked teasingly, and the breath caught in my throat. Hadn't I said similar words to Ian not that long ago when we were kissing and fooling around?

I remembered Ian telling me that time in the spirit world was different than time as I knew it. I didn't want to wish for something that couldn't be...but I had to wonder now exactly what he'd meant.

I stared at him for a long moment. He tilted his head to the side and grinned, and I swear I saw Ian in that smile...and in those long-lashed, brilliant blue eyes.

Flustered, my gaze fell to his necklace and my heart skipped a beat. "I have a cross necklace with the same Celtic design," I said, reaching beneath my shirt and showing him.

My palms started to sweat. What were the chances of that?

"See, now you really must accept a ride. We're kindred spirits."

Kindred spirits?

I liked that.

Kade shifted on his feet, and I realized he was waiting for my answer.

"Sure, I'd love a ride," I said with a smile.

His grin was devastating. "Let's go," he said, his long fingers sliding over mine.

I turned, and that's when I saw her, standing right in the middle of the road, as solid as any of the kids rushing across the schoolyard.

I felt the blood drain from my face.

It was Laria...and she was staring directly at me.

Also available from

D. A. Templeton

The Haunted (a MacKinnon Curse novel, book two)

The Departed (a MacKinnon Curse novel, book three)

The MacKinnon Curse (The Beginning) novella

Acknowledgements

Thank you to my critique partners, T.R. Allardice, P.T. Michelle, and Beth Ciotta, for taking time out of your busy schedules to give me insightful feedback. I'm forever grateful for your help and your friendship.

To my family—for supporting me in every endeavor I've ever had. You've been incredible cheerleaders, and you're at the heart of everything I do. I love you!

About the Author

J.A. Templeton writes young adult novels featuring characters that don't necessarily fit into any box. Aside from writing and reading, she enjoys research, traveling, riding motorcycles, and spending time with family and friends. Married to her high school sweetheart, she has two grown children and lives in Washington. Visit her website www.jatempleton.com for the most updated information on new releases. She loves hearing from readers!

CPSIA information can be obtained at www.ICGtesting.com
Printed in the USA
LVOW11s0915121014

408392LV00006B/850/P